Tobias Carroll

IN THE SIGHT

WHISKEY TIT

VT / NYC

This is a work of fiction. Names, characters, places, and incidents are the product of the author's imagination, and should not be confused with your idea of reality.

Resemblance to actual persons, living or dead, events, or locales is entirely coincidental.

Published in the United States and Canada by Whisk(e)y Tit: www.whiskeytit.com. If you wish to use or reproduce all or part of this book for any means, please let the author and publisher know. You're pretty much required to, legally.

ISBN 978-1-952600-41-8

Cover design by Matt Lyne.

TOBIAS CARROLL

~1~

Farrier had been raised in the East, and that aspect of his life persevered in how he thought of distance. Consider this night: nothing on the road ahead of him for miles and nothing behind him on the road for miles. Nothing to either side except the numinous hills and outstretched farms. Occasionally he'd see a lit window in a farmhouse and imagine the resident there, a scion or spouse of some forlorn farmer up late with a television program or tattered publication, following someone else's story into the small hours. On most of these drives, Farrier crossed distances that would have spanned several states in his home region. Here, he'd be lucky if he crossed one border.

He'd made his peace with that a long time ago.

Solitude on the road somewhere in the eastern half of Nebraska. Off in the distance were lights, a strong enough beacon that someone unfamiliar with the road might take it for a small city a dozen miles off. Farrier knew better. All that was there was a large service station, usually with a few short-haul trucks parked in its lot and a small convenience store with surprisingly good coffee in its carafes. He had stopped there a hundred times over the last few years, and could summon the late-shift staff's faces from memory. None of them ever acknowledged him, which seemed fair. Anonymity served him well.

Right about here was his favorite part of the song emanating from the car's speakers, where the singer's register shifted and the singer's voice cracked and the whole thing rose from introspection into a louche glam-rock splendor. Had it been warmer outside, Farrier would have rolled the windows down and sung along, but on this particular night, he opted out.

On the passenger seat was a box and in the box was an object and at the gas station in the distance was the person to whom he would deliver that object. This was how tonight would go and this was how nearly every one of these nights had gone for the last decade, ever since he had moved to a small house in the Midwest, bought the materials needed for his work, and gotten to it.

Farrier was the last extant member of what could be called a secret society, had its members sought to dub themselves that, which they had not. Farrier had nought to do with that decision, made years before. Had he been consulted, Farrier would have argued that the term "secret society" carried with it a sort of currency, and thus could be used for purposes of achieving a certain desired outcome, to wit: secret societies got you things. Secret societies opened hidden doors and revealed mysteries, holy and otherwise. Without that designation, they were simply a collective of eccentrics, tending towards the potentially criminal. Was there a word for a plurality of eccentrics, Farrier wondered, in the vein of a murder of crows? He'd need to look that up when he reached shelter for the night. Research was for steady moments and solemnity. He was not there yet. Here was here, in a place where things could still go wrong.

That part in the song's chorus that he liked came around again. He turned up the volume. The roads were still barren and the fields were still silent.

One summer when he was twenty-one, Farrier had been on a late drive home after some social outing. He'd been young and broke at the time, which was why he hadn't sought a night's lodging at a motel rather than simply continuing home on cup after cup of rest area coffee. On this particular night he had lowered his windows and let the rush of air from outside bombard his face. He had turned the car stereo up as loud as he could without drowning out the sounds of the road, and from time to time he sung along with the songs that emerged. He knew his tricks for staying awake at such an hour. Ten miles from home, he'd passed by a familiar passage of landscape; a bridge over a reservoir, followed by a series of tall trees. But his mind had glitched; in sleeplessness, he saw those trunks as the legs of an impossibly massive wolf, and some primal part of his brain took this sign as that of a predator. He saw the shape in the distance and imagined that creature leaning down and, in one motion, gulping his car down its maw. Young Farrier knew this was impossible, knew that his lack of sleep hadn't somehow transformed his familiar world into one of monsters, and yet, his pulse quickened as he approached, and he held his breath as he passed below.

The trees had remained trees, and his car proceeded without the marks of teeth several feet long. Still, ever since then, Farrier had vowed that he would find a place to sleep on the occasion that he ever found himself similarly deranged. Farrier had a decadent tendency, true, but he preferred control over his own hallucinations; he preferred to manage his mind's own sorties. In his own roundabout way, he believed in precision.

Since then he'd become the final enduring member of the secret society. They'd gone by many names, most of them delivered with a jester's solemnity: the New Bygones; the Unsleeping; the Shadow Parliament of Cumberland County; the Mammoth Three. Farrier had briefly worked with a group of chiptune artisans headquartered around here. He delivered the segments and they delivered the money and that was, in effect, that. And so, he believed, this night would go. The gear was different; the product was born of a different technology, intended for different ends. Back then it was engineering and now it was pharmaceutical. It was a low-risk production from either approach.

⁂

Twenty minutes of barren road later, he was there; his driving was at an end, for at least a few minutes. Some gas stations illuminated the landscape around them, as if they were themselves palimpsests of light bulbs. There was a steadiness to them that suggested a kind of shelter, a kind of way station, to those standing in the vicinity. Not so here. This place had patchwork lighting; it forked and flickered in places, suggesting nothing quite as much as the last service station before the end of the world. With the proper repairs, a steady and consistent light seemed possible. Farrier had never seen this be the case, however; not here.

Farrier stepped out of the car and stretched his legs. He had arrived early; he generally did. He began to pace in the parking lot. Long drives took more out of him these days. As he'd crossed the threshold of forty he had begun to notice his body disappointing him: a frequently sore back, and certain stabbing sensations in his shoulders. So he'd started booking rooms in hotels with gyms along his routes; he'd endeavored to rise earlier and spend time putting his body through its paces.

There was a dormant truck in one corner of the parking lot, and a pair of recent-vintage sedans fueling up. Farrier edged closer to the actual building. In one hand was a bag and inside the bag was the stuff. He wore a nondescript grey jacket, as anonymous a look as he could hope for. He stepped through the front door and saw the usual guy working behind the cash register. Otherwise, he was alone there. And so he decided he would kill some time.

Farrier browsed the store's aisles and saw the usual selection of packaged foods designed for road trips. He always hoped that he'd see something that broke through the theme of standardization; he hoped that he might see something strange, even if that surrealism came solely through the form of a regional potato chip flavor or some locally-beloved fruit or cheese. So far, he had not discovered such a thing, and he didn't hold out much hope that a wholesale changeover of this particular outpost's merchandise had occurred since his last visit.

After fifteen minutes of wandering through the aisles, Farrier checked his phone again to make sure that no one had called. He decided to wait outside. He bought a cup of coffee, liberally added milk and sugar, and went outside to drink it. He was halfway through the cup when the pickup rolled in, and Farrier knew in that moment that his time had arrived.

Since the last time he'd seen the pickup, it had gotten a new paint job. At least some of it had: in the low light of the parking lot, it looked to Farrier like only about half of the hood had new paint on it. The rest absorbed light and seemed to be in a state of perpetual shadow. He'd ridden in there once, with a man who only wanted to talk of his diorama hobby. It was menacing, though – Farrier had been left with the sense that, had he not been appreciative enough of the art of diorama, he might well have been ejected from a moving car, left to fall on the side of the highway, left to be ruined by whatever came next.

The song he'd last been listening to on the drive here came back through his head on another loop. This was how it was going to go, he realized. He'd end up enmeshed in another awkward convalescence if he wasn't careful. He recalled the last time that had happened: bandaged and herbed in someone's back room, periodically shouting — half-delirious and half-ironic — about this thing called modern medicine, about these things called hospitals. But his clients would have no use for that. Periodically someone would read from scripture or New Age tracts, or a builder of dioramas would sit and explain the mathematics behind scaling something down. It wasn't his favorite, though he did budget for those pauses, time and money both. This was a line of work that involved some broken ribs, some concussions; this was a thing where one could only be aseptic for so long.

The man who stepped from the pickup's cab this time had a familiar look to him: a kind of football hero gone to seed, it seemed, with a later-in-life endeavor to become intellectual abandoned after a few weeks. In other words, this was someone who could harm Farrier in unspeakable ways and who might, in the midst of some crisis between quarterlife and midlife, have written a sonnet about it afterwards. Just his luck, Farrier thought.

This man's face was neutral and guarded. You could never be sure, Farrier thought. Some of the clients he met were practically bubbly after the exchange had taken place; others turned hostile or self-loathing. Farrier had never quite pieced together an overarching theory of their behavior. For a while he had taken it as a given that the clients who were middlemen were more cautious, while those who planned to make use of the product themselves embraced them. On a rainy night near the border he'd been disabused of this notion. It had been the only time he'd ever been chased after a handoff: four hours of watching his rear view mirror until he felt he had shaken them.

It was an occupational hazard. Farrier wished his compatriots in the onetime secret society were still available to him, but: no. They had all left that life behind.

The large man from the truck gestured towards the windows of the shopping area, and Farrier nodded. Generally, both Farrier and his clients preferred to be somewhere in view of cameras, for a sense of mutual security. He feared no ill consequences here: there was, after all, nothing technically illegal about this transaction. Here they were, two old friends, one handing the other something they'd misplaced. For all anyone else knew, that was the interaction.

So: back to the neon-lit retail space, the night outside hazy through uncleaned windows. Farrier introduced himself to the man on the way in; the man offered up the name of Calvin. Whether that was name or alias, Farrier neither knew nor cared. Inside they browsed a bit. Farrier preferred to keep these interactions casual, to blend in with the surroundings. Calvin thumbed through a selection of snack-sized chips before setting on a small bag of roasted pumpkin seeds. Farrier bought a bottle of seltzer. Normally he'd have preferred caffeine, but his hotel wasn't far off, and he liked the idea of sleeping once his body hit the bed, rather than the alternative.

They paid for their goods and stepped back into the parking lot.

"What can I expect?" Calvin asked. So it was for him, Farrier thought. Most of his clients didn't tip their hat. This man had been the factotum for an earlier client, and had now bought into the product Farrier was selling. He was not the first to go adjacent to the stuff for a while and eventually become intrigued. Farrier was unsure if there would ever be a last.

"It takes about fifteen days," Farrier said. "First five, you'll feel mostly like yourself, just with...additions or subtractions. Last five, you'll be whoever you become, more or less. It's the middle five that tend to be rough. Bits of the two of you fighting it out. If you can, I'd say, find somewhere quiet to relax — a cabin, or a hotel where they don't check in on you too often."

Calvin nodded. "I'd heard about the same."

Farrier just nodded in return. The nature of the stuff made that tricky; he could never tell if those who'd used it were subtly fucking with him, or with those that sought out their advice, when they praised things to high heaven. Still, the transaction had gone through and the handoff was underway. So that was calming. And then Calvin said something else that fucked it all up.

"A fella named Hal told me to tell you something, " Calvin began, and that was around when Farrier started to feel sick. "He said to watch yourself, and he said not to go home. Not this night, and not any other. He said you're a target now." And with that, Farrier froze to the spot with bile in his throat. Calvin continued down the parking lot towards his pickup. "Hail and farewell," he said, stepping and letting a residual wave go before he entered his car.

Farrier stood there for the next ten minutes in silence. It wasn't an instance of him gathering his thoughts or trying to plan his next step; rather, it was that cold feeling of panic that flooded him. He was too panicked to properly panic; his fight or flight response needed time to even kick in. And then it did, and he sprinted to his car, knowing all the while that he looked ridiculous. That part from the song that had been stuck in his head came back to mock him; it looped again and again whenever he thought himself tranquil, and he spent much of the night crouched in his hotel room's chair, feeling chilled and creaky. As dawn broke, he called the front desk and extended his stay by a night; he pulled the drapes and the blackout curtains as closed as he could, and he began a sleep that would last for most of the day.

~2~

It was past four in the afternoon when Farrier rose. He spent an hour in the hotel's gym, reviving muscles gone slack from driving, then returned to his room and packed. He checked out and was on the road by five thirty. The sun had mostly set. Here he was, keeping vampire hours again. Driving down this stretch of interstate summoned flashes of the last time he'd been here. He kept seeing echoes of the same scene: a couple arguing roadside, who always seemed to be in the midst of a heated quarrel as the lanes of traffic sped by. It struck him as strange at the time, to be honest. Sometimes you'd pass one car on one stretch of highway and then see the same car fall behind you forty minutes or two hours later, and you could chalk up the discrepancy to one of you having stopped for gas or food or a scenic outlook. Here, though, was this couple: a woman in a deep green dress and a man, entirely bald and clad in a leather jacket, raising his hands in a gesture that, in another context, might have been perfectly suited to some arcane ritual.

He'd passed them playing out this bizarre scene no less than four times over the course of three hundred miles. And then, fifty miles later, he saw the woman in the deep green dress walking on her own on the side of the road, her estranged beau long gone.

Farrier understood back then that there was a logical explanation for this, as well as about half a dozen illogical explanations. Still, he wondered what other strange things he might see by the side of the road on this trip, and how many he might have made along the way.

What Farrier wanted right now was somewhere to sit and read and ponder his options. He recalled one such space, the Interstate United Reading Room, six hours east of here. He'd met its builder once: Emilia Kopel, architect and libertine, obsessed with creating spaces as habitable for the spirits of the dead as they were for the bodies of the living. They'd spoken at the same event once, a long time ago, before a time when their interests had crossed from the esoteric into something else. Still, they'd hit it off. Farrier maintained a membership there, and so he'd have access, along with coffee and an isolated alcove in which he could sit for hours and chase the dawn, if he so desired.

So that was where he was headed.

Farrier didn't miss the industrial parks of his youth. They were inevitable in his hometown: boxes and windows in abundance, potential golden ratios all the way down stubby streets that ran perpendicular to the county highways and state routes. Sometimes he went to spend the day with his father at his office or his mother at her office; as he grew older, he ended up with summer jobs in some of them, filing mail or moving office equipment. Once he'd had a temporary assignment clearing out a factory that was relocating to another country; once he'd spent weeks cataloging and carefully wrapping antique furniture. *The suburbs are where national splendor goes to die*, a friend of his had said at the time, a de facto kid brother named Andre King. Last Farrier had heard, young Andre King had become a secondhand client of Farrier's product and had remade his life. Farrier wondered if he'd even recognize Andre today; it had been decades since then, and he might have opted for some other name, Irving or Mitchell or Travis. Such was the state of things.

Emilia's work on the Reading Room wasn't really visible on the outside. She fucked with the insides of spaces. That was her trademark, albeit phrased in less profane terms. From the outside it looked nondescript, like a sales office or a warehouse or a furniture showroom. A packed house full of accountants; a distance learning center; an ill-starred cooking school. Ten, fifteen years ago that had certainly been the case. Here and now the Reading Room sat in the same complex as a craft brewery and a space in which those who offered up twenty dollars an hour could throw hatchets at plywood. The parking lot was largely empty; Farrier's car's headlights illuminated one bumper sticker that read "I [heart] Late Capitalism," which struck him as far too direct. Then again, Farrier had never been one for bumper stickers, tattoos, or t-shirts that featured any sort of text. All of them played out far too closely to confessions for his liking.

Farrier stepped out of the car and walked towards the front door. He had a Reading Room key in his pocket. He intended to be there all night, and he had the next hotel in mind. Above him was a clear sky, stars, and a half moon. He heard something, and looked back towards the building. As he walked towards it, a woman left the front door and made her way right, headed to one of the handful of cars present in the lot. Farrier squinted. The height was right, as was the body language — she could well have been the one he kept seeing in the midst of roadside quarrels, and then, afterwards, walking alone. A double, another echo, or the progenitor; Farrier wished he knew. He was close enough that he could hail her with a yell, but he feared what might come next. Instead, he brought his key to the lock and made his way inside.

~ 3 ~

On earlier visits Farrier had seen the Reading Room packed and cacophonous, a sort of grand festival in miniature. He stepped inside and had to brush past bodies standing and seated, each of them consulting some document, whether paper or electronic. It wasn't his ideal working conditions; there was always someone there to ask him about something pressing or strike up a casual conversation. Once he'd walked inside on a brightly-lit afternoon, the sky outside as beatific a blue as he'd ever seen, dotted with a transcendentalist's clouds. It had been years ago, that visit; long after he'd met Emilia, but a time when the product and the business were both recent.

He started making his way to a preferred room of his, one with a piss-poor view of the parking lot outside and a paint job that seemed half-assed when compared to the neighboring rooms. Farrier liked the weird places, the places that seemed underdone. They were usually quiet, if nothing else.

So Farrier was on his way to the room when he felt a tug on his elbow and he turned. The man who'd sought his attention was a diminutive man with nondescript hair and a magnificent moustache, and this man asked Farrier if he happened to know where the bathroom was or, barring that, if there was an attendant on duty to whom the man with the moustache might pose some questions, nominally for research. Farrier answered the second question first: there was, in fact, no one on duty there; that was the point of the reading room and was part of the nature of its role as a private club. There was a form of security for it, but that was arcane; and besides, Emilia had never explained that part to him and he had never asked, because he was, fundamentally, a responsible adult.

Farrier posed a question back to the man with the moustache: how had he come to be here without knowing certain essential facts about the nature of the space? And the man with the moustache said that his memory of the last few years had been shit, that he'd discovered the key while cleaning his home and knew what it was for, but knew nothing else save that it afforded access to the Interstate United Reading Room. "I have a lot of gaps from back then," the man with the moustache said. "I think I did a lot of things I'm better off not remembering."

Farrier processed this for a moment and the man with the moustache looked at him askance and repeated his earlier question about the bathroom and Farrier paused for half a second, resentful that the man had interrupted him on the verge of assembling two and two, and directed the man with the moustache to the bathroom and thought some more, and then began to shudder. He'd seen the man with the moustache before, only then he'd been bald and clean-shaven and had completely different mannerisms.

Usually Farrier was good about recognizing former clients. That this one had changed so much left Farrier unmoored. It was in that moment that Farrier got the first glimpse of the full scope of this thing, and trembled a bit more before making his way to the room with the mediocre paint job. He was here to sit down and chart routes for deliveries and investigate certain figures who'd hoped to join his clientele, to embrace the product, but all that he could think about was the time he'd met the bald man, the man who'd taken the stuff that caused him to become the man with the moustache.

The bald man had been a friend of a friend of one of his partners, had seemed entirely jovial and content, an academic with a sideline in experimental music. They'd stood out in the backyard of some Seattle bar during one conference or another — Farrier always blended in at conferences, for whatever reason — and compared notes on mutual acquaintances. The bald man was likable enough, though evidently not so memorable that Farrier would remember his name. But here was the first indication that his worlds might overlap, that one of the people to whom he'd sold the product might have passed it along. It brought together the world of the secret places he stopped on his travels and the world of the product and the clientele, and the mess he was in now.

.*.
**

He was nearly alone in the Reading Room on this night. He could sit in any room he liked, even one with a good coating of paint.

So. He had been at this for eight years now, occasionally caretakering near the Boundary Waters or in northern Wisconsin, but largely sticking to his home base. He had a fixed address but it was unimpressive. On certain days, from the road, he'd have deliveries sent to that address, books and records and trail mix. He liked the idea of knowing that there was mail waiting for him somewhere. It was one of the handful of ways in which he allowed himself to be sentimental.

He thought again about the message he'd been given in the parking lot in the middle of nowhere and wondered if that home address was even viable anymore.

He punctuated the air for a moment, poking at something in midair, something basically nonexistent.

This was how it went: Farrier and his two cohorts made their madcap secret society and then they discovered the product. They'd gotten into varied things, most notable among them body modification for purposes of mood modification. If you had the right gear, you could solder together something to control a mild electrical current to the brain of whoever was connected to it and, ostensibly, lead them to a point wherein they no longer felt such a pronounced sadness. They'd gotten into that in college. Others enjoyed MDMA or weed or drugs more pernicious; for them, it was about the science. And the bliss, of course, but it was a scientific sort of bliss. Absolutely. Science in your bliss, or bliss in your science. Who could deny the appeal of that?

This was how it went: Farrier and Lopez and Erskine, researching all sorts of things and assembling chemical cocktails and endeavoring to rewire their own headspaces. Erskine even got a grant for some of it, which impressed the other two to no small extent. This work continued for several years, long past their collegiate beginnings. They had a small warehouse and a small salaried cohort. They worked within their means.

This was how it went: the time Farrier wondered about neurology, about case studies of people whose personalities had changed radically after some sudden and possibly traumatic event. And the time Lopez looked into questions of random number generation, and if there wasn't some possible way that the brain could be utilized to reflexively generate a random number, around which some structure could be built. And the time Erskine's fieldwork led him to substances that destabilized certain parts of the mind, and a whole body of research surrounding that. And the time Erskine spoke of a friend with severe depression, who wanted simply to be someone other than themselves. And the time Lopez spoke of the properties of cognitive-behavioral therapy and hypnosis and the science behind how they worked. And the time when Farrier stayed up far too late one night, poking and prodding at certain compounds, and greeted his partners in the morning, the two of them well-rested and Farrier haggard yet ecstatic, Farrier grinning, Farrier saying, "I think I've got something.

This was how it went: the realization that a compound, a substance, a drug that effectively turned you into someone else, was probably not the sort of thing that was viable from a commercial standpoint. Nor was it legal. Still. That was how it began. And now Farrier was all that was left of it: never skint, but always solitary. A compound, a substance, a drug, a product. His product, and his circuit to deliver it.

This was always how it went, until it wasn't.

*
**

Since that tripartite epiphany, they had been discreet. And then, when it was down to him, after his collaborators set out for more lucrative and legally permissible avenues, he had been especially discreet. But the message he'd received in the parking lot in the middle of nowhere indicated that things had, somewhere, gone south. His options were limited. He had two deliveries left before he'd need to return home and manufacture more product and head out again, and both of those were still a few days off. But this was what he missed: the sense of comfort that he got from those gas stations in isolation, the festive and familiar warmth of corporate color palettes. The message had left him all fucked up, to speak crudely. These next two handoffs would be unfamiliar and fraught. There was little to look forward to.

As he sat in the alcove of the Interstate United Reading Room, he ran down a list of all of his past clients. His relationship with them was a sort of one-and-done scenario: he handed the product over to them and handed over a sheet of instructions, and that was that. Over the years, a handful of clients had informed him afterwards that they had opted not to consume the product. Some feared the change; for some, the presence of the product was a kind of revelation, a reminder that perhaps the changes that the product promised were not ultimately for them. Farrier had a specific list of directions for how the product could be destroyed. He asked for some proof of its ingestion or its destruction, and none of his clients so far had failed to do so. The implications of what might happen if the product was released into the wild fundamentally terrified him.

He wondered in that moment if the product had finally backfired; if it had turned someone relatively peaceful into someone who thrived on conflict. He imagined a lunatic postcard arriving in his mailbox; he imagined someone fully formed after the fifteen days the product took to reach its full effect, and that person remembering only his name and a seething hatred. He wondered if that was how it would all go, if that was how it would end.

Not long after he'd sat down in this room, he'd heard the front door open again and someone, presumably the man with the moustache, making their exit. Now, in the midst of his reverie, he heard the door open again and a set of footsteps making their way into the building.

Farrier heard deep breathing, the sound of a physically large man with more than a little phlegm rattling about in his throat. He heard the steps before he saw the form obstructing some of the lights from the room that led to the room in which he sat. Into the room briefly stepped a man. This man paid Farrier no mind.

The man had short dark hair and the residue of childhood acne on his face. It was severe: rather than empathy for a stranger's awkward adolescence, Farrier briefly wondered if some pitted statue had been given life and was now wandering these shelves and desks. In one hand the tall man held a worn and ill-folded road map, the sort of thing purchased at a distant gas station a decade ago. The man's breath sounded — there was no other word for it — wracking.

Farrier felt unnerved. He'd been experiencing these bursts of fear: that some faceless figure had it in for him, that he'd awaken in a hotel room to see some form in silhouette looming in the corner. This man, though, would have been a fearful sight devoid of context in almost any space. He looked like a bouncer who could petrify with a stare, or someone who could be cast as the heavy's henchman in a cult action movie. Farrier felt that way before he noticed that the man was bearing a sledgehammer.

The huge man didn't acknowledge Farrier sitting there, mulling over his options. He was discreet; he seemed the very paradigm of etiquette in such a space, letting everyone else go about their business while he went about his. Still, though: the hammer, a massive thing as tall as a fifth-grader, its head roughly the side of someone's housecat. Farrier couldn't not monitor the man..

The man with the hammer walked to the wall twenty feet from Farrier, planted his feet, and then swung the hammer into it, then swung again, and again. The wall was marred now, with three distinct holes; pockmarked like some lunar surface. The man with the hammer turned and walked left, away from Farrier. There was a small circular window that, on his visits here, Farrier had thought of as a kind of porthole. The man's walk ceased. He steadied himself and shattered the window deftly, then moved into the room from which he'd come.

Farrier could hear the sound of collisions from there as well: some, Farrier thought, must have been with the walls. There were also more solid connections followed by the sound of objects falling, which must have been the destruction of several pieces of furniture. What left Farrier unnerved most of all was the spacing of things. This was not intended as demolition of the reading room; this was certainly vandalism, but it wasn't wholesale. It was a teaser for future destruction, a proof of concept.

Farrier stood but remained hunched over his chair, frozen, until he heard the sound of the door again and could be reasonably sure that the man had gone. He waited until much later than that before he finally left.

~4~

Farrier left the building behind after twenty minutes or forty minutes or two hours. It would be hell for whatever builder or designer had to work around the damage. From what he knew of the space, some sort of security would be there soon. He had no real interest in talking, or filing a statement, or answering a couple of questions. So it was only him here, alone in this parking lot, a sparking lamp overheard providing the only illumination for miles.

There was no sign of the hammering man and no sound of a car in the distance, either departing or approaching. This, at least, calmed him. He headed north.

The road was dark on each side of his car. As he glanced right and left he saw a handful of buildings, all lights extinguished. He'd known this look from driving through resort towns in the off season, that sense of a place fully enveloped in slumber. Most anywhere else, you could see at least some signs of life: the lit window of an insomniac, a light on in the home of a late-shift worker, a drunk coming back home after last call on their front porch, letting the night suffuse them and bring them back towards sobriety.

This was a ghost of a town, or a town's failed reflection.

Ten miles down the road he saw a light, and when he got to that light he saw that it was a gas station with a statue of a dinosaur out front, which looked familiar. Beside that he saw a hotel and outside of the hotel was a gleaming metallic rocket. That was some symmetry, Farrier thought. Both of them looked sleek; both could easily have served as hood ornaments for some other era's vintage automobiles.

The hotel was more like a motel, and had little to draw Farrier's eye save its existence. He inquired at the front desk as to whether a room was available for two nights; it was, he was told. He inquired at the front desk as to whether there was anywhere to exercise; the weight room was under construction, he was told. He inquired at the front desk as to whether there was anything else open around these parts; there was a bar around back, he was told. They weren't particular about their hours.

He crossed back out to his car and looked up. There it was, next to the motel sign in broken neon: the word BAR, the tubing shuddering and striving to flicker. He needed to plan a next step, and this place seemed better than a hotel room, where he'd inevitably start feeling constricted. The shape of hotel rooms did that to him sometimes when he was at peak stress. He had cultivated this life to reduce his total stress, and now it had all gone to shit.

Back home Farrier had a minimal will, which specified very little other than a request that he be buried in an ovular casket. He was unsure if such things existed, but he hoped that they might. He had read somewhere about a service that would use your corpse as the base of nutrients for a tree, and that sounded all right to him as well.

The bar was small but about halfway full, which struck him as the ideal level for a bar. He sat down and ordered a lager and realized after a few minutes that the bartender resembled a former client, and that struck him as a terrible potential turn. Or maybe he wasn't; maybe this was just someone's 70% doppelganger, and he could leave it at that. Farrier kept his head down. He hadn't heard from Emilia, which he hoped meant that she wasn't blaming him for the catastrophe at the Reading Room.

There was a beat-ass popcorn machine in the back of the bar, and Farrier walked to it and refilled a shallow plastic oval there three times over the course of the next twenty minutes. He devoured the stuff, sometimes pulling out individual kernels and directing them to his mouth and sometimes pulling out huge chunks of and funneling them into his craw. He was aware that this was potentially grotesque and he didn't much care. It was a way to spend the night, and he was nominally on the run.

After ordering a food-based cure for the road's delirium, he drank his night's last drink and walked back to his hotel, locked the door with as many locks as were available, pushed a chair up against the door in the shittiest of blockades, and let slumber take him. The last thing he remembered before sleeping was the realization that continuing north was a bad idea and that he should shift directions when he next hit the road.

⁂

It was by the third night, and the second arcane hotel, and the third low-slung bar, that Farrier was honest with himself and acknowledged that he was avoiding cities on his route. Some of this came from ingrained habits, as his meetings and handoffs generally happened in liminal spaces in the middle of highways somewhere. But some of this came from the particular feeling he got in cities.

He remembered a day when he'd felt spent by mid-day and had opted to nap for a bit. He'd awakened after two and a half hours when he'd hoped to be dormant for a third of that. So he'd gone out into the city and roamed the streets. It was a little after eight, and the sky was already dark, and that was part of it. His body still felt taxed, but he had somewhere to be, and so he was venturing there. It felt much later in the night to him, though. It felt as though he was brushing up against bars' last call; it felt as though, had he looked at the sky again, he'd see the first telltale signs of morning there. He'd felt as though the day and the night were both lying to him.

That had been years ago. Now he felt like that in cities all the time. It had been brewing before that, but then the sensation had clung to him, like some sort of vengeful ghost. Farrier's fondness for open spaces wasn't necessarily based on a love of them quite so much as a sense that they were necessary to how his mind functioned. in another world he might well have been hopelessly agoraphobic outside urban areas, with fields and farmlands as toxic to his head as any proper poison.

He sometimes wondered what would happen if he partook of the product, if he could simply rewire his own brain so as to skim away this bizarre divide, excise it in the name of progress. But he knew that it wouldn't work like that. The product kept certain things the same — it never affected sexuality or gender, to cite two examples — but otherwise, nearly all aspects of one's life were fair game. But then again, the clientele — the very small, very select clientele — were all people who'd gone beyond simply being dissatisfied with their lives. They were fed up with their very selves, and this was a way for them to change that.

Farrier was panicked and on the run, for sure, but he wasn't nearly at that level of disquiet.

So here he was, in a hotel room somewhere in western Kentucky, trying to suss out his next step. And his next step seemed awful to him, because his next step was to rush into a city and see where it led.

⁂

He was closest to Nashville, but even Nashville seemed impossibly huge to him. So he needed to warm himself up; he needed to become inoculated. Those old tiers of acclimation, slow and steady and never not nightmarish. Usually it was three or four days on the outskirts of progressively larger and larger boroughs, eking himself towards downtowns. Even then, he preferred to keep odd hours, small hours. What he wanted was all-night diners and shops in small alcoves; what he dreaded were drunken crowds or people who might otherwise accost him, press up too close, say *what brings you out this late, you some kinda vampire, nah I'm just playing with you, I know you're not a vampire, but you'd better not bite me, you know what I mean, because I kill vampires, you know?*

This hadn't happened to him yet, but still he feared it, or something resembling it. It was among the reasons he kept to himself: that unsettled fear that he got when he encountered someone wholly irrational. Even his own practice, so strange to some as the bygone trio explained it, was still based around science. Science and a randomly generated process for sure, but still: science. Observable characteristics. Results that could be repeated.

They'd begun with homemade electrodes, brief shocks to the brain to alleviate depression and bring them closer to the transcendental. That was how it began, homebrewed head science.

In those days, Farrier missed the point when they were still adjusting their own brains. But he also understood why that part of it had ceased. There needed to be some sense of consistency. There needed to be a level wherein each of them understood that they were the person they'd been the day before, the week before, the year before. Farrier embraced this, and his cohorts had not.

Their names had stayed the same, but neither of his former colleagues was recognizable to him any longer. They were still civil, of course, like members of a band who'd stuck together for the cash and otherwise loathed one another. He'd last encountered Lopez on the outskirts of a Nebraska mall eighteen months earlier. They'd conversed below a tall sign with a glowing screen. It had been one of the worst conversations of Farrier's life. He wasn't sure if it even dented Lopez's resolve.

So what was left? He passed a cluster of national chain stores. He had a soft spot for the coffee at one of them, but continued on. He was thinking of finding a place to take a night in Clarksville. He'd never even passed through, but it struck him as manageable. As long as he couldn't see the downtown from his room's window, he'd be all right.

~5~

Edwin Hollister was the first. Farrier barely knew him; he was close to Lopez and Erskine. Edwin was a broken-looking man, like an Egon Schiele portrait pulled from a canvas and left to wander around campus, some post-graduate revenant who struck some as irresistible and warded away others. Farrier and Edwin were at the status of acquaintance where they'd nod knowingly to at parties, where they had enough in common that they could maintain a functional conversation at various and sundry social gatherings. That was all right by Farrier. Farrier had few close relationships. He wasn't exactly estranged from his family, but he also rarely spoke with them or saw them. This was true then and it was truer now.

So Edwin had apparently murmured to Lopez once about a grand feeling of discontent, of estrangement, of alienation. About wishing to change himself on a fundamental level.

"You could exercise more," said Lopez.

"Change your style," said Erskine.

"Find a quality therapist," said Farrier.

Edwin shook his head. No, he told them, it was deeper than that. It was a fundamental disconnect with who he was, with the shape of his world. He wanted to become someone different, a sloughing off of his very self. "Reincarnation," he said, "but without the death part."

Edwin had been around for some of the trio's earlier experiments. He was discreet, and discretion was necessary. These tasks were, after all, not strictly legal. There was the potential for harm. And while Lopez and Erskine had quietly fucked with their own minds here and there, they had never fully immersed themselves in it. There were others they'd treated who'd undergone various processes to a much more substantial extent. Not so the trio; not so Farrier, especially.

It was a gorgeous campus. Trees planted in symmetry and a neat cluster of red brick buildings and another neat cluster of newer buildings built with glass and steel that rose several stories higher than their neighbors. And in the distance, a student center, and further in the distance, a small arena. In the autumn it was a gorgeous space in which to simply sit and absorb all those pastoral emotions. And in the spring and summer, the look of green leaves on the trees and the smell of the grass and the sounds of a hundred heated conversations lent the area a vibrance that never failed to energize Farrier. It was the last time in his life that he truly felt comfortable around that many people.

But here, too, he began to discover his fondness for furtive spaces, beginning with the one he'd helped found with the rest of the trio, their quiet center for brain science. There were other such rooms, one made by a sculptor named Deepa and one made by a bartender named Allen and one made by a biologist named Hank. Hank's was the weirdest of all, as she'd fucked structures and essentially turned the bottom floors of a house she apparently owned — Hank came from a well-off family — into an immersive and immensely artificial biodome of sorts, in which real fauna and artificial creatures intermingled and, occasionally, tore one another to pieces. It was a strange sort of bloodsport, or would have been had the bloodless automata ever been on the winning side of the perpetual conflicts.

Edwin and his misery continued, and the secret society debated what could be done for him, and to him.

Three months later they had something. Initially there were three pills, to be taken in weekly intervals; eventually Farrier and Lopez and Erskine got it down to one pill that made its changes over the course of fifteen days. They fed Edwin the first pill and told him to come back in a week and told him to come back in less than a week if he felt strange in any way.

They didn't hear from Edwin at all in the first week. On the first Monday after they'd treated Edwin, he showed up for the second pill.

"How are you feeling?" they asked him. "Better?"

"Better," he told them. They ran the usual tests on him; he showed no sign of ill effects. Some of these tests were physical, while others were psychological: asking him to find patterns in an image, running word associations, asking him about preferences in music, in sports, in potential travel destinations. They recorded these results and compared them with the baseline results, taken before Edwin had taken the first pill. They showed little change.

A week later he returned for the third pill. "How do you feel," they asked him.

"Bicameral," he said.

"That's good," they told him. "That's how you should be."

Farrier paused and broke from the group. "Is it manageable?"

"Mostly," said Edwin. "Sometimes it's like I'm listening to headphones with different music coming over each channel."

"Give it another couple of days," Edwin said. "It'll pass."

They ran the same tests with him before giving him the next pill and sending him on his way. His body remained exactly the same. His word associations, his preferences, his yearnings — all of these had drifted from their baselines. There was hesitancy, though; sometimes he'd say one thing, like an indication of Portugal as a desired destination, and then walk it back, shifting his preference to be a voyage to Saskatchewan instead. This, too, was as it should be.

On the third Monday, Edwin walked in.

"How are you, Edwin?" they asked.

"Revised," he said. "I like it."

The tests proved out what they'd expected. Physically, this new edition of Edwin was the same man as the one who had come to them seeking assistance. Psychically, he was wholly different; the changes he'd been drifting towards a week earlier had solidified. This was a new man, but also not.

They told Edwin to contact them if he experienced any strange sensations, shook his hand, and bade him farewell. And that was the last they'd heard of him.

~6~

Eighty miles outside of Nashville was the sole North American retail location of Il Zacala, an Italian chain that combined a handbag retailer with a coffee shop. It was open for twenty-two hours out of the day and was rarely full. Farrier had once read that this was a benefit of the shop's proof of concept status: it was run at a loss despite rapturous coverage from retail publications worldwide, and a cult following of food enthusiasts who delighted in a certain array of pastries available there and only there.

Farrier was fond of the place. He pulled into its parking lot shortly before midnight. It stood alone, its neighbors mostly warehouses with minimal activity at that hour. And then there was this small structure, evoking a classic diner but with a forest green color scheme around the perimeter, the front window holding a handful of the company's offerings, its illumination a strange beacon in the night.

The interior, as always, was spotless. The retailing side of the space occupied about two-thirds of it. As he walked through the door, Farrier could see row upon row of handbags tastefully arranged and a clerk in a tasteful uniform positioned halfway between the door and the back wall. Farrier headed left, into the cafe. Here, hardwood furniture and a long counter awaited him. Here too was a store employee, this one working as a barista. Sitting at the bar were two men whose similar appearance and ages suggested a father and son or — this seemed less likely — two brothers of wildly disparate ages. Farrier sat down and ordered a coffee. He left the family a wide berth and began thumbing through his phone, looking at email and maps and notes from previous trips, trying to pinpoint the exact place in which the city's pull would begin to make him tremble.

"Excuse me," came a voice from behind him. Farrier turned and saw the younger of the two men standing there. He looked to be a young fourteen or so, his face christened with inexperience, but the bottle of imported beer before him suggested that he had a young face more than anything.

"Yes?" said Farrier. He was reasonably sure that these two were not secretly agents of those who meant him harm.

"My dad and I were wondering," the young man began, and then stopped. Was he trying to figure out how to phrase something, Farrier wondered, or was his question something inherently awkward? Farrier hated that moment where a sentence shifted, when contempt might be revealed.

The kid just let it hang there, though. Finally Farrier closed the circle. "You were wondering what?"

"Oh!" the kid said. "Right. We were wondering if you're in a band."

43

This wasn't the first time Farrier had been asked that question. "I'm not," he said.

"Were you ever in a band?"

"No," he said.

"You're absolutely sure?"

"I'm absolutely sure."

The kid nodded his head. "Well, okay." He returned to his meal. He took a bite of his sandwich and then looked back up. "I'm sorry," he said. "That was rude of me. I should have mentioned that this line of questioning was due to the type of work that my father and I do. We are in the business of entertainment law. It is how we conduct ourselves. And thus when we saw someone who looked to be keeping odd hours arrive at this place late, with a solitary cast to their face, well, I sought to inquire. "

"Well all right," said Farrier. "Do you have a card?"

"I do," said the kid. He tapped his father, who until that point had been methodically eating his meal forkful by forkful, on the shoulder. He whispered something to the older man, who reached into his coat pocket and produced a silver case. The older man opened the silver case and produced a business card. The older man handed it to the younger man, who handed it to Farrier.

Modal Enterprises, it read, with the usual information. "Thank you," said Farrier. "If I run into any musicians, I'll pass it along."

"Much obliged," said the kid. "We're soon expanding into corporate law. Helping companies go public, that sort of thing. Diversify the business."

"Well," said Farrier, and paused. "Well, that's never a bad thing, is it?"

"No sir," said the kid.

Farrier finished his coffee, paid, and left.

The hotel this time was squat. No fitness center, no bar, no attached restaurant. There was a pool, but it was drained, with an adjoining sign speaking of repairs and promising an improved aquatic experience in the months to come.

Farrier checked in, carried his suitcase to his room, and closed the blackout curtains. Tonight he decided that he was going to DIY his brain in some unspoken way. He was unsure if this would involve a tincture of some sort of simple electrodes; he only knew that he needed to fuck with his head in some fundamental and unfathomable way, and the fact that he had a portable selection of tools for this very purpose revived him.

After the secret society had fallen apart, he had consulted briefly with a technologist, Mara, who spoke repeatedly about the idea of versioning. Personalities as operating systems; and thus, Farrier's chosen discipline considered as a series of upgrades.

He'd never been able to make sense of it, but then, he hated computers and software. Perhaps that was another reason why he was on his current path..

Farrier had never really been into senses of chemical highs, alcohol and coffee excepted. As he withdrew the minute case from his suitcase, he pondered how he'd gotten to this point: DIY brain manipulation in an anonymous hotel room in the middle of nowhere. He'd had stranger weeks, but none quite so filled with dread.

He connected one device to the room's speakers and brought up some music: a repeating cyclical thing, more waveform than pop song. This was how it always started for him, on nights like these. As he slid the device out of the case he checked its charge; it had been months since he'd last used it, but the meter indicated that its battery was around two-thirds full. That was a good sign. He affixed the electrodes to a pair of points on his skull and let them settle in before pushing the button for the first time.

This was a timed thing, a sequence. Some people meditated; Farrier sent pulses through his brain, a targeted sequence. It wasn't ever entirely painful, but it still tingled. The sounds playing gave him something steady on which to focus, gave him something into which he could slowly immerse himself.

This was the other part: on one level it didn't hurt and on another, it hurt quite a lot. Quick jolts, again and again.

He'd tried it once without the steady pulses and waves, only the sound of a television, and he found himself terrified at the point when he realized that he was losing language, or losing his ability to distinguish phrase from phrase. From the television he had heard someone saying "what you own," or possibly "what you are," and he realized that he could no longer tell the difference between the two phrases whatsoever, and the possibility that he might lose this ability to distinguish between two similar but wholly different phrases — these two and so many others — left him utterly chilled.

On that night he had ultimately pulled through, with language again retaining a degree of clarification out of the skewed notes that had run through his brain during the process. It wasn't long — ten minutes, or perhaps fifteen — but he always wondered if this would be the last one, either by choice or through some defect in the machine which would leave it or him incapable of functioning. It cut through his thoughts like a guitar solo artificially raised on a mixing console; it was like a tiny dashboard Jesus mounted on the inside of his skull, preaching only to him in some pre-human language.

Farrier dreaded these moments, but he also embraced them.

With each pulse came the sensation of something being torn back and then instantly and seamlessly replaced. There was a steadiness, and there was a measured quality to his presence in the room. He sat there in the chair and heard the low sound around him and felt increasingly detached from his body, like he might simply slip and slide out of it, or like it might slip and slide out of him.

Finally he felt the sensation inside of his skull abate and heard the patterns and the waves around him slim down and eventually become nonexistent. He reached up to pull the connectors from his skull and was relieved to find them still there, was relieved that his fingers still came to rest on skin and hair. He had developed a series of fears around this process, not all of which were anything close to rational.

He sat in the chair for a little while longer. Eventually he stood, took a few sips from a bottle of water, and stepped out of the door and into the wider world of the hotel. He often felt restless after these sessions, and this night was no exception.

⁂

He decided to scout out the hotel's fitness center. He traversed one hallway towards an elevator and took that elevator up three floors and got out and traversed another hallway until he was there. Its lights were dim, and a hastily printed sign on the door advised that it was out of service until further notice. Farrier had little better to do, and so he looked inside through the window.

From what he could tell, each and every piece of equipment within the hotel's fitness center had been destroyed, with the resulting debris re-arranged in skeletal patterns across the floor. Farrier was impressed, in his own way: it would have taken a substantial amount of brute strength to destroy these machines, and an equally laudable sense of proportion and aesthetics to scatter and arrange them in this particular manner. They looked like the broken remains of some lost and harrowed creature; they looked like something alternately whimsical and horrific. Farrier spent twenty minutes there; the process with the device always left him fixated on details, and he was already prone to fascination.

Farrier walked back to his hotel room in lieu of a better decision or a proper destination, and when he got to his hotel room he saw something taped to the door and a surge of panic filled his body. He walked towards it faster and began scanning the hallway for sinister glowering figures in the style and mode of the man he'd encountered in the Interstate United Reading Room. He saw no other person in the hallway and saw no other shadows cast in the hallway, and his panic subsided.

The note was written on a piece of hotel stationary and had been folded over. Five words had been written on it in neutral block letters:

FARRIER

HOTEL BAR

BLUE SWEATER

It seemed self-explanatory to Farrier, and so he ventured towards the bar to look for someone in a blue sweater. He wracked his brain to ponder whether or not he knew someone in the area; no names or faces came to mind. This region was new to him; he had never traversed these roads before, and had little experience on them. No clients had drawn him here, and no old friends or collegiate acquaintances called this area home. He'd never been brought here, not by the secret society or familial ties or any other errand or task, related to the product or otherwise.

~7~

When Farrier was a child, he had briefly become obsessed with gardening. His parents cleared him a small dirt square in their backyard and lined it with bricks. He bought a series of seeds from a nearby store and buried them at the appropriate depths. He watered them steadily and regularly. He kept track of the small green shoots' arrival. He took a handful of photographs with the family's Polaroid camera. He was proud of this, was young Farrier.

Half of the garden was flowers and half of the garden was vegetables. Young Farrier did not cook, and thus the appeal of planting herbs did not occur to him. He monitored the growth of these spring plantings as best he could, and when the vegetables first began to bear fruit, he was gladdened. But before they could be consumed, the arrival of insects left them devastated. He found small devouring creatures on the outside of squash and tomatoes, leaving none outside of a state of fundamental ruin. He pondered alternatives for the following year: root vegetables were ruled out due to the neighborhood's abundance of moles and rabbits, and there was little space in the family's house for indoor growing. Had Farrier been decades younger, or had he a child of his own with similar inclinations towards agricultural cultivation, hydroponics might have been an answer, but the era of his birth neatly ruled that out.

Still, he had learned something from it: he knew from an early age that he craved control over certain spaces, and that his work could only properly congeal within them. In that, then, it was a template for what followed. The home he had left behind was a meticulously maintained space, one in which he could do his work with few obstructions. It was never less than spotless. It was, he sometimes thought, why he preferred hotel rooms when he traveled. For him, sterility in spaces, or at least a tactile sameness, was a laudable goal.

Farrier had read somewhere that this hotel's bar was open far later than most, that it hosted a music venue, that it was, unlike so many of its cousins, a proper destination for the residents of the area around it. On a normal night Farrier would not have gone to the hotel bar, and particularly on a night like this: adjusting his brain, making himself sensitive to certain details and emotions, never blended well with intoxication. Farrier had his preferred routines; tonight's destination was not a part of any of them.

There was no one in a blue sweater at the bar at the time of his arrival; nor was there anyone clad in a similar garment in the lobby beside it. And so Farrier walked in. There was neon along the walls, and a selection of artwork adorning an array of skateboard decks that ran towards the back. The bar itself was on the right side, and a handful of tables adorned the opposite wall. Farrier saw one large group that appeared to be the aftermath of a wedding, judging by their attire. An obvious inebriate was gesturing angrily near a woman wearing an ornate dress, who was gesticulating back with a corresponding air of fury. Fancy dresses, well-tailored suits, but not a sweater in sight. Farrier found a corner of the bar far from the larger group, signaled the bartender, and ordered bitters and soda. It was his default drink for situations like this. He retuned his brain with some regularity; tonight's spell was a special occasion, but it wasn't so close to the previous process that he felt alarmed.

He was halfway done with his drink when he saw something blue out of the corner of his eye, and slowly turned. Standing there was a woman apparently in her mid-20s — though Farrier had a long history of estimating ages incorrectly — with short hair, thick glasses, and an aquamarine sweater. The bar's lights reflected in her glasses, completely blocking his view of her eyes. It was, for Farrier, a disconcerting sight. Eyes were something he could understand; losing that was an unknown, a mystery. And mysteries were something Farrier endeavored to minimize as much as he could.

53

She saw him and began walking in his direction. This answered the question that had hung in his mind since he'd arrived here: did whoever had left the note know what he looked like? Evidently the answer was yes. She approached the bar, sat on the stool beside Farrier's, and signaled the bartender. She ordered a neat pour of a peaty Scotch, took a sip, and then turned to him. "You're Farrier," she said. "Emilia sent me."

"Do you have a name?" Farrier asked.

"Ms. Gibbs will do for now," she said.

Farrier had never heard Emilia mention a Ms. Gibbs, but that hardly indicated anything. Emilia kept certain aspects of her life and work well under wraps, and his conversations with her had always encompassed a narrow range of subjects.

"So, Ms. Gibbs—" he began.

"I'm here because of the shitshow at the Reading Room, your room number wasn't easy to pry from the front desk, and your route's been simple enough to chart," she said. "I find people for a living and you remake them. I can't quite decide if that makes us natural enemies."

"What is it about the 'shitshow at the Reading Room' that drew you here?"

Ms. Gibbs took another thin drink of her whiskey and looked back up at him. "I tell you this because we're not adversaries, at least not right now: you should know that there's a security system there. What did you expect would happen if things went awry?"

So this was new. "What happened to the other man who was there?" he asked. "The hammer guy."

"A colleague has been tracking him," Ms. Gibbs said. "He's nowhere near here right now." That, at least, was reassuring.

From across the room came a wet sound and then a concrete sound. Farrier turned and saw the bride standing over the drunk man with whom she'd been arguing earlier. "Come on, motherfucker," she said. "Say one more word." Normally in these situations there'd be someone being held back. This was not the case here; there was only a woman in elegant lace garment, her knuckles bloody, looking for a reason to kick a drunkard in the face. Farrier turned back to the conversation.

"What are you drinking?" Ms. Gibbs asked. "I'll get you something."

"I'm not drinking anything," he said. "Just seltzer." The interaction in the bar was beginning to make his skull pulse.

"Come on," she said. "Really? You have a reputation, you know."

This, Farrier was pretty sure, was bullshit. Still, he felt compelled to explain something. Confessing that he'd DIYed his brain earlier seemed a mistake. "I'm feeling ill," he said. "Under the weather."

Ms. Gibbs nodded and took another drink. "Hotels will fuck you up," she said. "Especially the family ones. Kids everywhere. Breeding ground for germs. I've got a room but I'm not actually sleeping in it."

"Fair enough," said Farrier.

Ms. Gibbs drank again. Farrier noted that he was hardly drinking his seltzer and bitters. This didn't unsettle him. "So what about the whole thing has you entranced?" he asked her. "What brought you all the way out here? This information could all come through a text."

She nodded. "Emilia wanted me to give you these," she said. She reached into her back and withdrew a massive golden envelope, the sort of thing architects might use to circulate blueprints. "This," she said. "She wanted me to give you this. Which I'll do at the end of the night. If we left it on the bar it'd only get soaked. Someone's spilling a drink tonight. Maybe not you or me, but someone."

"What's in there?" Farrier asked.

"Magazines," Ms. Gibbs said. "From Emilia's collection. Suggested career changes. Vacation plans. The usual. She does love giving advice."

All Farrier could manage here was a low rumble from the midpoint of his throat. This was not wrong, what Ms. Gibbs had said. In all of his time knowing Emilia, she had frequently shared her opinions on most aspects of life, of his chosen vocation, and of his potential alternatives. She wasn't shy about it. That was likely why they so rarely saw one another; that was likely why they were communicating now via proxy.

It struck Farrier in that moment that he had very few people he could consider friends. He wasn't sure if it was sentimentality or the aftereffects of altering his brain or some strange memory that the presence of Ms. Gibbs at the bar was summoning up. Had he been drinking he would have chalked it up to the accompanying melancholy, but that was clearly not the case here. Still, he felt stung by the realization.

"Are we done here?" he asked Ms. Gibbs.

"We're done if you want to be done," she said. "I'm going to stick around a bit. Maybe the fighting will start back up."

"It's going to be an early morning for me," he told her. He wasn't sure if this was true. Nevertheless he bade her farewell, received the envelope full of magazines, and walked back towards his room. He glanced back once at a distance of forty or fifty feet. She was still at the bar, having ordered a new glass of Scotch. The wedding party continued to dance in one corner, and the drunkard rested in another, a bag of ice draped over his head. Ms. Gibbs took it all in, and even as Farrier watched her take in the room, he had no doubt that somehow she was watching him as well.

~8~

For the rest of his stay at this particular hotel, he found no notes affixed to his door or slid under his door or wedged into the crack beside his door. He was fine with this. With a night of sleeping his head felt thoroughly neatened and compartmentalized. That, too, was good. He woke early, donned a swimsuit, and headed for the pool, where he swam his body clean as best he could.

Soon enough he was back at his car, luggage in tow. Here, too, he was pleased to discover a dearth of notes or other communiques. He sat in the driver's seat and readied himself to start the car and then paused. It was then that he remembered the oversized envelope that he had received the previous night. He smirked at the comical size of it, as though it was a normal envelope designed for some bizarre race of giants. He rolled down both of the car's windows and allowed himself a moment to breathe some air. It was clear here; there was little pollen that would clog his nose or spawn wracking coughs from deep within his throat.

Farrier tore into the top of the envelope and the seam crumbled like attic rot. Fine, he thought, reached in, and withdrew what appeared to be local travel magazines, the sort of thing you'd pick up at a rest area in an anonymous part of the country, advertising local harvest festivals and canoe trips and the ideal hot-air balloon ride to take to see fall foliage. Farrier had taken one of those once. He'd been on a date. It had gone well, and then it had gone horribly, as the two of them had discovered that they were not remotely compatible. On that particular evening Farrier had been told that he would be alone forever, and that tag had stuck.

All of the magazines looked past their prime. He checked the corners of the covers and saw dates that were three, four, eight years gone. At first he hadn't the slightest idea what this all meant: Emilia had always struck him as a good communicator, and these were decidedly random. These were the gifts of a surrealist or someone undergoing a breakdown; these in no way left him with a sense that she had a plan, or a point of view, or a perspective on such things.

His first move was to rifle through their pages, to see if something was marked within. These seemed random to Farrier, but he'd grant that there could be a cipher buried within, or a note made from excised words, or a composite diagram arranged from disparate pages. Instead, he noted slight bulges in each of the four magazines, as though something had been inserted between their pages. His fingers sought it out in the first periodical and he gingerly withdrew them, grasping a flexible grey sheet of some unknown material. The display looked primitive, and yet not. He set it in the sun and turned his attention to the second publication.

This, too, held little except for a similar grey sheet. This, too, was withdrawn and left on the seat. As he set it down, Farrier saw something in the first one: a handful of words were dimly visible on it now that it had been sitting in the sun for a few minutes. The grey of their font was largely indistinguishable from the grey of the material, thus making the words virtually illegible, but still. After repeating these withdrawals, Farrier lay all four on the dashboard and waited for them to receive enough sun to offer up some sort of message. In the interim, he stepped outside of the car and walked around the parking lot in circles, his old method of head-clearing finding new life in this space.

The previous night's conversation with Ms. Gibbs, and her talk of enemies and compatriots, reminded him of an earlier trip when he'd provided a checkup to an old friend. Revaz was his name, a childhood chum whose acquaintance with Farrier had endured into adulthood. Revaz lived on a farm in the middle of nowhere, a ten-minute drive through unlit roads after one left the highway. It was the family's business; Revaz hadn't exactly inherited it, but he was maintaining it while his parents traveled. Revaz was a tall and rangy man who never seemed entirely at home in any space, whether that was the suburban classrooms of their youth or this more rural setting.

Revaz had messaged Farrier and expressed some concerns about his memory. Farrier responded quickly; he was going to be in the area in a few weeks' time, and could visit him then. There were tests he had; supplements and devices that he could use. Revaz has acquiesced, and a time had been set for the two of them to meet.

This had been a few years ago, but even then Farrier was in the habit of driving wherever he could to deliver the product. Heavy rains on the interstate two hundred miles north had slowed his progress, and he didn't arrive in Revaz's proximate area until long after nightfall. He had called at one point, to tell him that he wouldn't be on time; he offered to spend the night in a hotel. No, Revaz had said, the guest room was all set up. He would be fine.

Farrier saw no other cars on the roads leading to Revaz's farm. He pulled in and saw the farmhouse: a low structure, made from meticulously arranged wood, several windows glowing from within. He shuttered his engine and withdrew his overnight bag from the car. Here he already felt secure. He walked to the front door and knocked a staccato rhythm. He could hear the approach of footsteps; the door opened and Revaz stood before him. The two had changed little since their adolescence: neither had lost much hair, and neither had opted for mustaches or mutton chops. They greeted each other with handshakes and Revaz ushered Farrier inside.

He learned things quickly: Revaz's parents, the fourth generation to run the farm, were traveling; Revaz largely lived here alone; there were two employees who would arrive early the following morning.

"The solitary life," said Farrier.

"Indeed," said Revaz.

"How do you like it?" said Farrier.

"If I'm going to be honest," Revaz said, "I don't all that much. But the alternatives aren't much better, and at least this is good for my health."

The thing about Revaz's place, Farrier noticed, was its asymmetrical precision. It wasn't just that the rooms through which they'd passed and in which they stood were clean, though they were; it was also that there was a meticulous order to them along with a sense of imbalance. These looked like showroom images where something had been added or subtracted to throw the whole space out of proportion. There were a half-dozen reasons Farrier could think of for this type of arrangement, and none of them warmed his heart. He was fine when he controlled something to the point of sterility, but he had little interest in immersing himself in the sterility of others, especially with these slightly dissonant signs.

They moved from this room and its pristine carpeting and its sharp-edged sculptures and its precision-molded wainscoting through a spotless glass door and onto the back patio. Farrier saw seats arranged around a fire pit. He assumed Revaz had stoked this in anticipation of his arrival. They sat for a while and spoke of their shared past. Neither addressed the reason for Farrier's coming. The night was clear, and the stars overhead reminded Farrier of why he spent most of his time outside of cities.

After an hour of conversation, Revaz indicated that it was time that he called it a night. "This life, " he said. "These hours." Farrier, no stranger to discernible sleep cycles, understood completely. He stayed up for another hour, then quenched the fire and walked to Revaz's guest room. It, too, was precise and subtly out of balance. Farrier's sleep was soundless.

The following day, Farrier unpacked his gear while Revaz worked on the farm. By three, Revaz was finished; he asked Farrier if he had time to shower before beginning the tests, and Farrier concurred.

Someone had once told Farrier that his gear for these sessions looked like the devices of an experimental musician. Someone else compared their spread to the instruments of a veterinarian whose practice involved resuscitating deceased housepets. The latter person had been stoned to the point of blindness, but it still left an impression on Farrier; to be entirely precise, the exact phrasing and tones of the stoned person's voice had become enmeshed in the back of Farrier's subconscious, periodically escaping to taunt him at inopportune times.

On that afternoon, Farrier had before him the following items: a deck of flash cards, a handheld air raid siren, a small box with three cables emerging from it, two electrodes connected to the box, an unstained notebook, and a fine-tipped pen for inscribing notes on the aforementioned pad. This was not Farrier's first time doing this kind of test, and he felt comfortable with the system.

When Revaz had first called, he had spoken of odd gaps in his memory: a handful of oblique scenes that seemed excised. He had compared the experience to blackouts from drinking, though Revaz rarely drunk those days, and never did so to excess. Needless to say, he was concerned.

This iteration of the test took twenty-two minutes to complete. Farrier noted no irregularities in Revaz's memory; nothing seemed out of sorts. From earlier records there appeared to be no cognitive decline.

Still, Revaz was worried. That night the two men sat out by the firepit and continued to talk about the gaps and the blackouts and what Revaz did and did not remember. It came down to this: it began during a fallow point in his business eighteen months earlier. There was little rhythm or pattern to it, like an infection that surfaced periodically to alarm and disorient. It was like something that lay dormant within him, Revaz said, something that kept its own timetable and awakened under its own volition. A form of psychic parasite, perhaps.

The blackouts left him feeling ruined. Not simply the lack of control, but the lack of knowledge. They sat there around the fire and discussed these things until long past midnight. Farrier had no conclusion he could offer; he had no treatment for such melancholy, nor for the symptoms that accompanied it.

As he sat in the guest bedroom later, Farrier pondered all of this. Revaz was one of his few remaining friends, and he was unsure of where this corridor of his life might lead. He had to be back on the road not long after he woke. That night he remained awake until the night sky outside of the window had begun to brighten.

He had a hastily made breakfast in Revaz's kitchen, packed up his suitcase, and walked around to the agricultural part of the property. There he saw Revaz in conversation with his two employees. He waved at Revaz, who shouted a hearty "Goodbye!" at him. And then he was off, back on the car and to his routine of dispensing the product along various highways and liminal spaces, and residing at anonymous hotels.

It took a week to realize that his supply of the product was smaller than it should have been.

He ruminated on this for the better part of a day before concluding something he'd have preferred to avoid: that sometimes while he had slept, Revaz had accessed his car and had pilfered a pill or two. One would have been sufficient; he was unaware of how much of the process Revaz understood. And so he called him once, then twice.

Revaz picked up on neither occasion. He waited a tense hour, then tried a third time; this time there was also no result.

The following morning Revaz returned his call with a chastened "Hello."

Farrier considered his words more carefully than he had pondered any in the past. "What have you done?" he asked his friend.

"I took it," Revaz said. "Two nights ago. I can feel it working."

This wasn't a shock to Farrier, but the news was no less brutal to him. "Fucking hell," he said. "Why?"

"This discontent," Revaz said. "The unrest. The sense of loss."

"You know what this will do," said Farrier.

"I do."

"Do you? You won't be the same person you were before. Talking about your work, talking about the business — the you that exists in twelve days might not care about any of that."

"I've written it all down," said Revaz. "I have papers everywhere. A cheat sheet for my life as it presently exists." And Farrier could imagine it, a series of stacks of paper, with meticulously arranged instructions printed on them: guidelines as to his identity, to how the business was run, to the important people in his life. Farrier had met people who'd spoken of trying to do this, but then, most of Farrier's clients were men not unlike Farrier: solitary, disconnected, unattached.

Farrier not infrequently wondered what would arise from him if he took the product. He wondered what that period of becoming someone new would be like; he wondered what it would feel like to feel his sense of self, and of his identity, slipping away. Or would he even feel it going? It might, he thought, feel only like a gradual displacement; less a sense of loss and more of a sense of replacement. He sometimes checked in with former clients: their memories were intact, and they understood what they had done. But even so, there was a sense of belonging, a sense of self-assuredness, a confidence that this was a feeling of destiny, that something outmoded had been replaced with something fresh.

Farrier wanted to say more to Revaz, but words failed him. He had no antiserum for occasions like this; he had no way to convince Revaz to purge what he had taken from his system. In this the die was cast, and he was at a loss. He had been tricked by an old friend, and his old friend would be fully reinvented by the end of the month.   In the end, all Farrier could do was wish Revaz good luck, in a halting and uncertain tone of voice.

In the car near the hotel, Farrier eyed the flexible screens that sat before him. All of them were now illuminated, and all bore short messages in text. This struck him as familiar;

he had read something about this technology on some website somewhere, sometime in the last seventeen months. He assumed, then, that this was also Emilia's doing; that he was being used as a kind of proof of concept.

That summarized his connection with Emilia fairly well. Theirs was a friendship based on a fondness for investigation, accompanied by the occasional provocation. And now the text on all of these had resolved into the same pattern: a sketch using text that resembled no one so much as himself. Each of them had the same pattern: a solitary figure standing on a hill, silhouetted against a neutral background.

Farrier's phone buzzed. On it was a text, evidently from Emilia. "You got my message?" it read. Farrier set his phone down, picked a direction away from the nearest city, and drove.

~9~

The Lifers' Bar dated back to the midpoint of Prohibition. It was on a side street in a small town; specifically, it was in the basement of what had once been a boarding house but was now a modest collection of office spaces. It was, not to put too fine a point on it, one of the weirdest places Farrier had ever visited. Over the years the local government had preserved it even as they enacted regulations and legislation that would make it impossible to replicate elsewhere in the town. It had been grandfathered so many times that its own genealogy was ornate and byzantine in the mode of cathedral architecture.

If the national government fell and the state government fell, The Lifers' Bar would likely remain intact. It had survived Prohibition and ill-starred moonshine and the time Oliver Hathorne's son had almost burned the place down. Walk in and you'd see a strange blend of the arcane and the modern, as though someone had moved a dive bar from the collective memory of Old New York and into this rural corner of the world. This extended to sawdust on the floor and open beams and staccato candlelights gleaming from table to table; it did not extend to the precisely miniaturized lights that nestled above the bar and above the tables, nor to the digital register, nor to the wireless speakers secreted in the rafters. The place only looked like it was soundtracked by a hand-cranked gramophone operated by a whiskered man who went by "Sully" or "Deschamps" or "Mulligan." But no. The wheels of steel were secure in a back room, a digital player governed the mood of the night, and the bourbon selection was second to none.

Farrier had arrived here in a taxi ninety minutes earlier. His hotel was a few miles down the road, but on this particular night he intended to drink himself silly. Perhaps not quite so severe, but regardless: he didn't want to have the potential of driving weighing on him as he drank, so he had taken it out of the equation. The taxi in which he had traveled there was only one in the most technical sense of the word. It had been a minivan operated by a woman who was driving her son back from a soccer practice. The kid sat up front with his mother and Farrier sat in the back, thinking back to his own youth soccer days and wondering just where everything had gone wrong.

He had been to the Lifers' Bar three times before. The first had been on Emilia's recommendation; the second had been for a brief meeting with Emilia, where they had traded policy papers and news of relevant technologies as candles smoldered on the tables around them. It had been a solidly okay night, in Farrier's estimation. The third time had been another night of drinking alone.

The name of the town was Vinstadten; some stranger had told Farrier years before that Swedes had founded the place, though Farrier saw no traces of them now. He had hoped for cured salmon or aquavit or reindeer meat on the menu somewhere in this town, but there was none of that to be had in the shops and markets of Vinstadten. And so he stayed at the chain hotel down the road when he was in town, and he came to this bar, and it left him largely sated.

Farrier paid cash for his first drink, something with applejack and aperol. He sat at the bar, four empty seats between him and the closest person, and nursed it. Emilia was fucking with his head and someone was dispatching people to fuck with him, period. He had some regrets, it was true. He took in the entirety of the place: there was a solid crowd, mostly couples and trios, all engaged in mid-volumed conversations. The bartender was bald and had a well-groomed moustache. The impression he was left with was of this place as a sort of way station, a place where groups went before or after certain events or meals. He was pretty sure he was the only patron there who was simply there for the night.

He assumed this place was safe; he assumed no hulking men would come here and begin smashing things. Then again, assumptions were what had gotten him here to begin with. He said a silent prayer and drank and kept his eyes on the door.

"Excuse me," came a voice from one side of him. Farrier turned and looked. Sitting there was a man of roughly twenty-five, a gentleman who looked like some minor aristocrat displaced from his usual private club or political chamber. It was this guy who'd called out. Farrier his eyebrows; that gesture was about all this guy was going to get. "Is your name Farrier, by chance?"

Well, fuck, thought Farrier. Another safe harbor to cross off his list. What did it mean to realize that you were in a space for the last time? His drink lost its flavor.

Still, he thought. The least he could do was glower at this dandyish man down the bar. "Who wants to know?" he asked, his voice heading in the direction of a glower.

"I've heard about you," the younger man said. And then he paused, adjusted himself, and stepped down the bar, reseating himself in the seat beside Farrier. "I've heard about you," he repeated, this time at a volume commensurate with their relative locations.

"What," said Farrier, "have you heard?"

The young aristocrat paused, then smirked. "You're not a person who has much use for contempt, are you? Because you don't fake it remotely well."

It was true, and it stung Farrier, which in turn brought an upswing of anger. That perfectly matched with a shift in the barroom's music: from an old-timey string band to Italo disco, that point at point at which the beat becomes synchronous and everything falls away. Farrier would have given anything to have been on a dance floor at that moment, and Farrier was a notoriously terrible dancer.

Even so, the younger man opposite him has caused his blood to boil, and while he was relieved to no longer be pantomiming contempt, he did think that he could muster up some genuine anger. And so he did, saying, "I may not have contempt on my side, but I've certainly got other things in no small supply."

The aristocrat smirked. "Is that so," he said.

"It is," said Farrier.

The aristocrat signaled the bartender. He pointed at Farrier. "This man," he said. "Whatever he drinks tonight? On my tab." And then he turned back and addressed Farrier.

"You're known here," he said. "Don't forget that." With that, he moved back to his original seat.

A malaise settled over Farrier as he sat there, doing his best to enjoy his drink, but failing at it. It felt like fog; it felt like something pernicious, a wall of static enveloping him, with just a tincture of screaming in the mix. It was an unwelcome feeling; it was a feeling that left him with the sensation of being the subject of a joke, or the target of a horrorshow of a prank, or a mistaken translation, a sense of two words or phrases carried somewhere absurd.

Still, the drink was good, and the ambiance was pleasant. But polite society would not allow him to simply mosey over to the aristocrat, grab him by his shirt collar, and begin to make demands. Demands in the vein of who the aristocrat was, and who was doing his bidding, and whose bidding he was doing. These might get him closer to his destination, or they might end him, and badly. To say nothing of the flaws that might emerge should the bartender, or a bar back, or some other employee of the Lifers' Bar reach out and 86 him from the establishment, and call local law enforcement, and raid the premises on which he stayed and search his vehicle and then, Farrier, assumed, throw him in the clink.

Farrier wasn't entirely sure that laws existed for the shit he was doing, but that seemed like a fraught way of going about things. He thought of cohorts of his who'd developed a penchant for DMT and how that had worked out. In a sense, he was treading on the edges of disaster. He liked the fact that he had a small clientele; he liked the fact that his clientele continued to be discreet even after they'd sloughed off their old skins and became new.

Not for the first time, Farrier considered his own endgame. He briefly looked at the aristocrat and cursed him for prompting these thoughts. Pondering his endgame never wound up well; largely, it involved imagining himself surrendering to trampdom, or in an orange uniform dwelling in a brick cell, or the obvious choice: isolating his supply of the product down to one pill, and then ingesting it, and waiting to see what mind emerged out of his mind, and waiting to see what it felt like to be replaced by some other version of yourself. He'd dreamt about this a lot; he would wake from dreams and knew that these were dreams set in a world where he himself had taken the pill and where he himself had become someone different and where he himself walked the earth in a fundamentally different configuration than his current one. These dreams left him destabilized for days.

Farrier wasn't the sort of person who normally used his phone at bars. He preferred the privacy and the constrained sense of sensory deprivation. Farrier had very particular thoughts about his own brain and the ways in which his own brain was stimulated and how his own brain might embrace something greater and something sharper and something more wonderfully precise. Back at his old home, in fact, at his old and potentially abandoned home, Farrier had a beloved hooded sweatshirt with a precise zipper running up the front and the phrase I BELIEVE IN PRECISION emblazoned on the back. Farrier didn't think of himself as the sort of person who had a favorite article of clothing, but this was clearly his favorite article of clothing.

Still. Tonight, he thought, fuck precision. He texted an old college friend, a marine biologist who'd spent the better part a decade living in Vanuatu in a state of relative isolation. Her name was Finch. They'd always joked that if everything else failed for them, they could always travel to Victorian England and open up a goods shop called FARRIER & FINCH. Owing to the lack of a time machine, this plan had failed.

"Finch," he texted. "I am at the bar in Vinstadten." He set his phone down and finished his drink and ordered another. When he looked down the bar he realized that the aristocrat had left. He hoped that this didn't mean that he was due to be jumped by the man as he walked out, but he doubted it. The aristocrat seemed like someone who got by on withering contempt more so than anything else. He ordered another cocktail, this one based around something that had been aged in a barrel.

"Hello Farrier," came Finch's response five minutes later. "There are many bars in Vinstaden. I assume you mean the one with the Prohibition cosplayers."

"Yes," Farrier typed. "You know me too well."

"You are a simple man," Finch replied. "I would join you tonight, but I am otherwise indisposed. Shall we convene tomorrow at the aviary?"

Oh hell, Farrier thought. The aviary. The thing about Vinstadten was this: after a group of enterprising Swedes had set down a handful of buildings, they had opted to journey west and thus left the town a preserved shell of itself. A wealthy trader named Hedland Alice had purchased the entirety of the town and had sought to build light manufacturing around it. Hedland's grandson, Phillip Gnomia, had grown up obsessed with birds; he'd been raised on Audubon guides as much as his mother's milk.

Briefly, Farrier wondered whether the aristocrat he'd spoken with was perhaps some lesser Gnomia cousin. It seemed plausible.

Phillip Gnomia had put his share of the family's fortune into a massive aviary just outside of the city limits. He'd populated it with a sample population of the local birds, and had gradually introduced species from further and further afield over the decade that followed. It had been a glorious regional attraction for many years; then, Gnomia had fallen ill during a trip to the Arctic in search of an obscure species of duck. His condition worsened, and that was the end of Phillip Gnomia. The aviary had gone to seed a few years later, some of its birds sold off to regional zoos and some simply released into the wild. The structure remained intact, however, and the local birds seemed to delight in it. It was a local landmark, albeit a tragic one. And evidently, a trip there was in Farrier's future.

_*
⋆

Finch was back here because she'd grown up here, and because she'd grown up here she had some stories to tell about life in and around Vinstadten. It didn't surprise Farrier to learn that the aviary was at the center of many bits of local folklore, urban legends, and campfire tales. The aviary itself was at the edge of a massive forest, and while efforts to landmark or restore the aviary itself had failed, the forest had eventually been deemed a state park and thus preserved from being turned into a development, golf course, or industrial park. For that, Farrier was grateful, and he felt that gratitude renewed on each and every visit he made to this part of the world.

Part of this came from the hollowed-out nature of the aviary's structures. Farrier had once read about the 1896 World's Fair, in which precisely and ornately designed buildings were erected but not designed to last, and there was some of that same ragged splendor here. The framework of the buildings had held up well over the decades; the walls and windows had not, and thus the effect created was one of huge impossible skeletons that refused to slump. The proximity to the wall of oaks and evergreens made this illusion even more pronounced, as though these buildings were the remains of some huge prelapsarian creatures that had lurched forth out of the forest, seen what humanity had made of the world, and promptly croaked.

That last image he'd stolen from Finch. She'd told him once that, growing up, she'd made up names and histories for all the beasts that rested here. At the time he had savored this small gem of information and had not asked the logical followup to it, which was to say, inquiring as to their names. He knew Finch well enough to know that she wouldn't react well to that, that she might smack him lightly, that the moment would likely be lost.

Farrier had pulled his car into a parking lot: there wasn't parking left for the failed aviary, but there was a small lot for campers and hikers making their way into the forest. He parked and walked away from the maintained landscape around the forest and into the weeds and dispersed trash that surrounded the aviary. From a distance he heard birdsong: nothing melodic or resonant, but instead harsh sounds, the sort of alarms that reminded you that birds descended from larger, fiercer creatures. He remembered Finch telling him that, in her youth, rumors flew about a population of feral peacocks that had roosted deep among the trees. She had, of course, dreamt of traveling into the woods and returning with one; it had only been years later that she realized that these rumors were likely ones that had lasted for generations, and would endure for generations more, and that the peacocks had likely become some grateful fox's prey by now.

Farrier walked along the periphery of the old aviary. He enjoyed this space. It was a way station of a sort, a liminal space unlike the liminal spaces in which he plied his trade. On some level, he understood that this was not a friendly space; on some level, he understood that these abandoned buildings might be home to actions or pastimes that would make him shudder or avert his eyes. Either way, this was a site in which he could lose himself. Here, he could stare at the decaying buildings and flaking paint and rusted metal all day.

He checked the time. Finch should have been there ten minutes ago, and it wasn't like her to be late. He checked the time again, and he checked for missed calls and missed texts. He checked his wireless connection; he had service. And so he continued his circuit and continued to wait. It took her another ten minutes to arrive: Farrier caught sight of a small car entering the same parking lot he had used and assumed that it was her, and then saw a familiar body exit the car and walk towards him. Farrier waved hesitantly. He certainly hoped that he was right in his assumption and that he wasn't beckoning to a stranger. It had been four years since they'd last been in the same physical space, and Farrier knew quite well the extent to which time could change someone. Changing people was his trade, but often time sufficed to do his work for him.

Finch drew close and spoke his name, and he said hers in response. They hugged; it was a warm and unambiguous greeting. Farrier had far too few people for whom that could be said. A brief and stricken thought ran through his mind: that Finch might well be the last person who knew him this well, and if she exited his life, there would be no one with that sort of proximity left. Even as he felt the warm familiarity of Finch's presence, this thought chilled him. He looked up and saw the skeletal ruins around him and wondered if that might not be his life at some proximate point. He wondered, once again, where all of this was headed.

"There was a man at the bar who knew me," Farrier said.

"You are there frequently enough," Finch said. "You're almost a regular, despite where you live."

"Not like that," said Farrier. "It relates to my ongoing troubles."

"That's a nice euphemism for it, Farrier," Finch said. "Are you truly fucked this time?"

Farrier sighed. "I have no idea," he said. This was true. This was either a temporary setback or his undoing, and as he roved the landscape his opinion of which one it was shifted between the two. Here and now, this blend of rejuvenation and despair didn't suit him. Neither did his lack of ideas. Ideas were nominally what had gotten him here; ideas had made him his way of living and had tripped him up, and now he felt spent.

He looked at Finch. "I think I'm truly fucked," he said.

⁎⁎

Finch never quite approved of his brain modification work. "One of these days you're going to damage something," she had once told him, and he was largely aware that she was correct. This was not a story that would end well, and yet. He was full-on *motorik* by now; literally all he knew how to do was keep moving forward, keep manufacturing the product, and continue dispensing them. At times he felt like a robot; generally those were the times he'd apply the electrodes to his scalp and let brief charges flow. He realized that this would likely seem insane to all but a half dozen people, most of whom were former colleagues of his in the secret society. Even so.

Now he and Finch were sitting at an archetypal diner on the highway twenty minutes from the shell of the aviary. He liked this place because it looked like every other archetypal diner across the country. As a child he'd gone to places like these with his family and had wished there was a system of connection between them. Step into one door in North Dakota and step out of it into an identical space in Florida and then step into a third identical space in Idaho.

Sometimes, when he thought about it like that, he wondered if the story of him and science really began there. It seemed a strange thing to build a life on, but it was far from the strangest thing in his life.

Finch was eating borscht, because apparently this diner had borscht on the menu. Farrier opted for a small cup of tomato soup and half a grilled cheese sandwich. Based on her reaction, it seemed as though Finch had made the better decision. He'd never been much of a borscht eater, to be honest. Much of this came from his childhood dislike of vegetables: cabbage and beets and spinach had been anathema to his younger self, and a weirdly primal distaste for them had persisted well into his adulthood. He wasn't entirely sure why, and he was entirely capable, even enthusiastic, about eating them in coleslaw or salads; just not in certain combinations.

He glanced out of the diner's window and felt a sudden surge of panic. Standing there was the giant looming man who had set upon him in the Reading Room. He looked at Finch.

"Something's gone wrong," he said.

Finch looked back at him. "Are you sure about that?" she said.

~10~

It seemed to Farrier as though they were clay targets, waiting to be cast out into the sky and then, oblivion. The diner's neon lights felt omnipresent and hotter than normal; they were akin to spotlights, turned on a convict just over the wall. The giant man still stood outside. He was in no hurry. The giant's gaze was on the front of the diner. Even so, Farrier felt seen in some fundamental way. He looked more closely at the giant. Under the giant's arm were a handful of folders bound together with something elastic. Perhaps he'd misunderstood the man, Farrier thought. Perhaps all he needed to do was hand over a real estate prospectus and the giant would be on his way.

He looked back at Finch. "So do you know him?"

"The ogre? No." There had been a time once, long ago, when he and Finch had regularly lied to one another. He was reasonably sure that they each knew the sound of one another's lies; he was reasonably sure that, in this instance, she spoke with unforked tongue.

"So tell me then," he said. "Why shouldn't I be worried?"

Finch cleared her throat. She tapped one finger on the edge of the table. It resonated nicely. These tables were well-made, Farrier thought, and then wondered why he was thinking that right now. His stray thoughts came at him in a deluge, and then he caught sight of some motion in his peripheral vision. The giant was headed for the door.

This was it, he thought. The point where all his shit decisions finally turned on him and rendered him down to something soft and broken. He felt few regrets, until he did. There was the point of cleaving himself from his onetime friends in the secret society; there was the moment when he realized that the product was far more valuable when sold illicitly than it would have been for him to take a legitimate line of work. There were friends abandoned and left incomplete and that telltale feeling of emptiness.

The lights felt even brighter on him.

Now the giant man was in the diner, and he walked effortlessly towards their table. He stepped towards them and stopped in front of their booth. His shoulders stretched the width of the table and the seats beside it. He was almost comically imposing, the sort of figure whose mere presence was likely enough to convince people to do his bidding. He loomed, and that was enough.

The giant cleared his throat. A low gravelly "Hmmm" emerged. Farrier tried to get a better look at the object beneath his arm, which was medium brown in color and box-shaped. It looked to him like the sort of accordion files he'd have seen in his parents' offices, or the sort of thing an accountant might embrace around tax season. An accordion binder was in fact what it was, complete with an elastic band holding the whole thing together. The giant set it on the table between Finch and Farrier.

"These are the names," said the giant. Farrier wished that the giant had a disproportionate voice to his frame, that he might squeak or sound overly congested or something that might detract from the air of menace, but there was no such out. The giant was huge and could likely crush Farrier's head in one of his hands. "You have a week," said the giant. And then he turned and walked away from them, and then out of the diner.

They saw him walk out through the window; he continued out of the parking lot and around the corner. They waited for a long time before they felt confident that he wouldn't spin around and return at a full run, perhaps to simply collide with the outer wall of the diner and leave it destroyed.

Finally, after a few minutes with their faces to the window in silence, they turned to face one another.

Finch pointed at the accordion file. "What the fuck is in there, do you think?" she asked.

Neither of them seemed particularly inclined to reach for it and open it.

Eventually Farrier did. It was an accordion folder with one pocket full to bursting with something long and bound, a small book or manifesto or prospectus. Henceforth he would think of it as the book, because that was how his brain was working on this particular night. So, the book. What was inside the book was surveillance.

Specifically, the surveillance that was inside the book was a list of names and a selection of photographs. The photographs weren't great; in fact, they looked to Farrier like copies of copies of copies, the faces' features sublimated into something monochromatic and brutish. Even so, he knew all of them. He'd handed each of them versions of the product. This was his clientele.

He explained as much to Finch.

"So they hacked you," she said.

Farrier shook his head. "No," he said. "I'm not so naive as to be that easily hackable."

"A break-in? An inside job?"

Farrier thought about it, but could think of no way in which his system could be cracked. Largely because there was no system. He maintained a slight cipher for his own records, but nothing quite so much as this.

He wondered just what the product had done to the man who'd gone after him like this, and who'd set this giant on his trail. He wondered what happened when you accidentally created someone who hated you; when someone's cure prompted the desire to gut the attending surgeon.

The materials in the folder were comprehensive. Inside was a list of each and every person who'd been reborn under the aegis of the product. It was a road map for something: an exposé or a criminal investigation or a series of targeted translations into something harrowing and disjointed.

There were no instructions in the book. Nothing inscribed on the pages, no notes clipped or pasted to the cover with staunch instructions. That would have been easier. Farrier could have handled threats or sinister communiques. This was simply a show of knowledge from an unknown point. And so that was where it left him. He understood that some unknown person could pull a dominance game on him. That seemed unlike how these things worked, but still.

He looked across the table at Finch. "What are you thinking?" she asked.

"I'm at a loss," he said. "I thought I knew where this was headed, and I don't."

She took a deep breath. "I think it might be time to fortify," she said.

"Fuck," he said. She wasn't wrong, but fortification was exactly what he'd been trying to avoid. Here he was circling Nashville in perpetuity, and fortification would require heading somewhere much larger.

"I know," she said. "I know."

All of the responses that came to mind were monosyllabic and exhausted. The following morning, he'd be headed for points north, two days of driving if he was measured and one if he was reckless. Right now, he felt reckless, though the truth of it was that he felt very little, and that felt far worse than recklessness.

After he'd bade farewell to Finch he'd taken the first few roads easily. There was little he could think about. His thoughts were concrete with slight shocks of panic erupting every quarter of an hour. The highways were eight-bit ghosts and the car ran evenly. The weight of the drive felt negligible.

Six months later he was adrift, living uneasily near the border between New York and Quebec.

~11~

The canal ran through the city, and the city was a college town, and the college town's life didn't normally impede on his dealings and thus he was fine with it. The city didn't set off his aversion to cities, it carried him along as he went. The city had buses that ran past his building every hour. Some of them rattled uncontrollably. They'd wake him from his slumber or send whatever dreams he was having into unpredictable and unseen realms. He was fine. He deserved it, he felt.

Farrier had a routine here, albeit a solitary one.

The building he was caretaking was owned by an old associate who'd bought the building as an investment and promptly forgot about it. So that was great. Farrier liked this feeling of being nimble, of living in the shadow of the affluent. He wondered if this was what the first mammals felt like. He'd been thinking about evolution for a few months now. He thought a lot about the way that science classified moments into eons, but how seismic change in an encyclopedia or textbook probably just looked like sunset and sunrise to those living through it. You slept, you woke, you did your business. Maybe after a few months you noticed that there were fewer giant lizards around. Maybe there was no visible change at all.

He would occasionally do odd jobs on the outskirts of town. He stayed as far from the university as he could. He had toured it once, in his younger years, and even when he regarded it from a distance it felt ominously familiar to him, like a comfortable shirt he'd been wearing his whole life. He wondered how far his old affiliations and connections might get him if he walked through their doors. Would he be embraced or demolished? Better to avoid the question, he thought. Better to avoid the temptation.

There was a guy named Gareth who rented boats and sometimes Farrier would take the boat into the lake between one border and the other. He enjoyed the idea of seeing the distant shore as something he could eventually lock onto and head for. It was an aspirational goal.

He had returned to his old home once and burned the bulk of his works back in the middle west. That, he thought, had been the end of it. He had repudiated the man he once was, had blacked out his name from numerous registers and allowed himself to sink into obscurity. This was fine. If he wanted to fuck with any other brains, his was present and available.

The college town suited him fine. He had still never visited its downtown, and the very idea of its downtown made his skin prickle. But he could sweep in on the fringes of it. He could sit back in a bar near the city limits and drink a beer in an outdoor space and gaze at the line of cars coming and going at rush hour and say, yes, this is where I am now. He was reasonably sure that if one more building over five stories went up, the whole locale would be ruined for him. For now, he could safely remain.

Some nights he called Finch, but those were rare and had become even more sporadic. Finch apparently had a gentleman caller, and Farrier didn't want to interfere in the courtship.

And then one day he received a phone call summoning him to Montreal. It was from that initial client of his, the one who'd summoned the giant to chase him. It was the changed man, the architect of all his troubles, on the other end of the line. How does one even have a conversation like that? How does one discuss the impossible? "Hello kind sir, I would like to renew our blood feud?" Farrier was in a position wherein he could be easily crushed. He knew it and his adversary knew it and he was at a loss as to where he should go next. He'd had stress nightmares more logical than that conversation.

The architect of Farrier's misery sounded like an agreeable guy on the other end of the line, which was perhaps the worst part of the whole thing.

"Mr. Farrier," said the architect of Farrier's misery. "We've met, but we've never met." This was an entirely true statement.

"What else do you want?" said Farrier. He was trying very hard to not sound petulant. As a rule, Farrier loathed petulance, especially his own. Nonetheless, he felt completely drained by this conversation, and this conversation had barely begun.

"I have a friend whose brain needs adjustment," the man said. He had been much less menacing when Farrier had met his previous incarnation. That man had been a meek man, a quietly broken divorcee who lived in a modest New England home and raised racing pigeons. Evidently, he'd been reborn as a crimelord, righteous and amoral. Had he been remotely interested in retooling the product's formula, Farrier would have taken this in mind for its next iteration.

Sometimes he would stand on one of the piers that jutted out into the river for no defined reason. He would watch upscale students in their boats rowing down it and he would smile and wave, pretending to be someone more affable than he was. One week he did that four days in a row, and when he sat at home the following day he realized that his inner ears were deeply off, that he now felt the water's sway beneath him even though he was on solid ground. Moments like that Farrier hated the water. He was tempted to call Finch and rant about the benefits of desert life. Then again, he'd never lived in the desert. As a child he'd visited Maine's desert, and he had flown over Arizona once. Otherwise, he had nothing to report.

⁎⁎

The first sign that things weren't going to go well was when Farrier asked the man in Montreal what he did and the man in Montreal said, "Hits." The man in Montreal, the contact from the architect of Farrier's misery — henceforth known as Mitchell — was a stodgy man in his late fifties. He wasn't particularly tall, but his shoulders seemed roughly as broad as his body was tall, and he carried himself with a poise that suggested a precise command of his own form, and a preternatural lack of body fat. Muscle, sinew, and bone; that was basically Mitchell's makeup.

They were on a ferry to Quebec City. Mitchell wanted to talk in relative privacy, and he assumed that this ferry would likely be free of professional rivals, law enforcement, and surveillance devices. It seemed to Farrier like a fair assessment. He wanted no procedures done to him. "I'm a DIYer," he said. "In the English manner. I take the plans, I make the thing, I apply it. You dig?" Mitchell spoke in a frenzied manner, like waves in some heightened tidal state making a rapid-fire battery against the shore. Here, Farrier was the shore.

At the ferry's concession stand, Mitchell had ordered two cups of tea. He handed one to Farrier. Farrier hated tea but understood that this was an instance where pleasing the client took precedence. He looked at the banks of the river and wondered what he had done to summon this inertia.

At a table inside, Farrier handed Mitchell plans for various devices for brain-fuckery. He reviewed each with him, detailing which components should be mail-ordered and which could be purchased at whatever the Quebecois equivalent of his local Radio Shack was. He told Mitchell what to expect from each device, and attempted as best he could to clarify when certain painful sensations were genuinely painful and when certain feelings of pain were a sign that the device was working. Mitchell nodded and asked few questions. Farrier could feel the swaying of the boat, and shuddered at what effect this would have on his equilibrium in the days to come.

By the time he was finished, they were nearly at Quebec City. Farrier and Mitchell walked out to the deck and looked out at the river and the banks of the river. It had been a moist day throughout the province, and mist rose up around the river. As he looked at the buildings built by the sides of the river, Farrier saw fog creeping in and advancing inland. It left him with a profound sense of disquiet.

The dock was visible now. "What happens now?" Farrier asked. Mitchell handed him a ticket.

"What happens now is, I disembark here, and you take the next ferry back to Montreal and go wherever," Mitchell said. "Our business is concluded. I hope you enjoyed the tea."

The tea had been garbage, but then, Farrier's expectations had been low.

Along with the other passengers, Mitchell and Farrier filed off the ferry. They reached the point at which they would part ways. Farrier was uncertain as to whether or not they should shake hands. Mitchell had seemed averse to physical contact for the duration of the trip, and Farrier figured that he would initiate anything if anything needed initiating. When they separated, there was no contact.

Farrier rejoined the ticket queue and purchased a ticket back to his city of origin. By the time he arrived back in Montreal night had fallen. He purchased a last-minute hotel room for the night and found a mediocre dinner nearby and slept fitfully. The next morning he woke, showered, and checked out. His breakfast tasted stale and lifeless. He was increasingly wondering what he was doing: he had foresworn his works and he had passed along information to a relative stranger, albeit a menacing one. He was unsure what the end product of this seclusion and this shedding would be; he wondered if there was anything beneath the layers he was sloughing off. Had he consumed the product, would he become someone else, or would he simply become no one, a fully blank slate for the world to batter for a while?

He boarded a bus and crossed the border back into New York. He was home before the sunset. He clustered in and opened a beer and sat on his front porch and watched nothing in particular happen. It was all right. A week later when he went to check his PO Box there was a check in there. The check bore the name of a former client, but Farrier was aware that the check was from the architect of his misery. The sum on the check was not obscene, but it was impressive. Written on the memo portion of the check were the words, "for useful consultation." It cleared with no issues, and soon enough he had a sizable amount in his checking account. The first thing he did with the money was to purchase a used car of a make and model that he'd heard was hardy. He was back on the road a day later. He stood by the canal and savored one last look at it, then entered the car and began driving west.

~12~

His westward drive took him along the banks of Lake Erie. He drove as close to it as he could, although he knew that this were not the most efficient route. Efficiency wasn't something he was particularly concerned with right now. His earlier journeys involved pushing against the night and brushing up against his own limits. Now, he was more unmoored. He had been broken and was now rebuilt, but in a much different configuration. He had become a different sort of vessel no.

He was motivated to drive and frustrated by driving. Had he been able to load his car onto a barge and simply take that from lake to lake and cover most of the country that way, he would have. Had there been an option to load his car onto a train and take that west, he might have done that as well. He remembered a north-south train with cars on it as a child, though he didn't quite remember the context. He might have been on it when he had been very young, or he might have simply seen advertisements for it on television at that age.

He hated that part of memory, the confusion of being told about a thing versus experiencing that thing. Idly he wondered if this was how he'd first been drawn to the mind and the ways one could manipulate that. He imagined a kind of filter that might retroactively separate those two kinds of memories from one another. But then again, was that something people would want? Was the idea of learning that a cherished childhood memory was actually a clever lie or a well-told tale all that beneficial?

At least the product had nominally been something that people wanted. As he considered it more, that sort of memory filter seemed to him to be more of a sham, a demonstration of his own cleverness with little thought to the consequences. This was the other downside of driving at this point in his life: that sense of being alone in his own head with himself.

He remembered that an old cohort of his named Washburn lived in the middle of western Pennsylvania. By some coincidence, he was not far from there now. He had spent twenty minutes earlier that day behind a buggy drawn by a pair of horses. The experience had been slightly infuriating but also curiously restful. He wondered if gas stations around here carried food items for equines. Unleaded fuel, ethanol, and bales of hay; all displayed, all for sale.

Near the border between Ohio and Pennsylvania he stopped for gas in a lakeside town. The overhang of the gas station spanned an octet of pumps; the small structure within housed a convenience store and a flower shop, and a chain pizzeria was a stone's throw away. At this point the hour was late. He decided to fill up his gas tank, eat unhealthy food, and find a place to rest his head for the night.

In the end he opted for an aquatic-themed hotel not far from a waterpark. It was the middle of the week; the hotel was largely empty. This was, as far as Farrier was concerned, good. The presence of parents around his age increasingly bothered him; he had never felt particularly called towards parenthood, but he'd also been left with the sense that he was missing some sort of life's purpose now. Before it had been the product, but now that was gone.

So what was the purpose of Farrier, at this point in time? This was what he was in search of. Washburn, his old friend, had always been a fellow traveler on the margins, involved in things that would soon be declared illegal but weren't quite there yet.

Farrier sat in the chain pizzeria and felt enveloped by false leather and low lights. He understood that this was an artificial evocation of home, and yet he was fine with that particular falsehood. The pizza had an absurd amount of cheese on it, and the meat atop it glimmered with grease. As he consumed it he could feel it come to reside in his stomach, like some sort of absurdist roughage.

His hotel was a Brutalist monolith, and for that he was grateful. He slept in, then went to the fitness center and worked himself to the point of painful sweat. He felt as though he was himself again.

At his hotel room's desk, Farrier looked at the late-morning light glimmering over the turbulent surface of the lake. He took out his phone and searched for Washburn's number. He dialed his old friend and waited for his voice, or someone's voice, to pick up.

***

Two days later, Farrier and Washburn sat in a car overlooking an office park in a suburb of Pittsburgh. Washburn had enthusiastically reconnected with him following his call. They'd met for coffee later that day, and Washburn discussed his current line of work. Like Farrier, Washburn had utilized scientific knowledge in the aims of ends that were somewhat frowned upon by ethics professors and law enforcement personnel. More specifically, Washburn was hired by largely amoral people to utilize low sonic frequencies to unsettle the minds and bodies of their rivals.

What this amounted to involved microphones and lasers and occasionally crawling behind the walls of buildings in order to install custom subwoofers and other bizarre audio gear. "I can beam the entirety of your favorite band's oeuvre directly into the skull of the quarry," Washburn said once. "Or your least favorite band. I'm not picky."

"But why would you do that?" asked Farrier.

"Maybe someone pays me to make someone hate their favorite artist," said Washburn. "You know that song 'Kokomo'?"

Farrier indicated that he was, indeed, familiar with it.

"This rich guy out of Edmonton told me his brother used to subject him to it every day when they were kids. Would just play it for eight to ten hours. Prattling about Aruba and Jamaica. So our man from Edmonton finally hits it big and decides turnabout is fair play. He hires me to find his big brother, who's now working construction on the Upper Peninsula. I head out there and scope him out and I wire every conceivable space in which he might lurk for sound. And I have the beaming thing, too. He even sleeps near a window, so I can beam the hip sounds of late-80s Beach Boys directly into his dreams and use his skull as a resonator."

"Jesus," said Farrier. "What happened?"

"Contract was for ten days," said Washburn. "So for ten days I did it, and then I broke it all down and headed home. The check from Edmonton cleared, and I was on to my next thing."

"You didn't find out what happened with the brother?" asked Farrier.

"Not my business," Washburn said. "I do the gig and I head home. Nothing more to be done." That, it seemed to Farrier, was Washburn in a nutshell.

They were outside of Pittsburgh for a similar task, something operational having to do with an auto body shop, a reclaimed piece of furniture, and someone's ruined reputation. Washburn had explained it all to Farrier, but he'd been quick enough with it that he'd left out a few details. The whole thing felt to Farrier like a beloved and byzantine novel that had been chopped down for an inevitable cinematic adaptation and lost a great deal of clarity along the way.

Still, Farrier was here. Washburn didn't seem entirely legit, but who was he to judge? Washburn had sham business cards with "The Grand Unmaking" emblazoned on them, which in no way seemed legitimate. And yet, he had his clientele. There were also kittens in his apartment, which unsettled Farrier. Washburn had never met a feral cat he didn't like, it seemed. There were four of them in Washburn's palatial loft; they had a separate room for their litter, which, Washburn had told Farrier, helped keep the odor confined and away from human possessions.

Farrier had many thoughts about this, not all of them kind, but largely let them slide.

They were in the parking lot of the industrial park because Washburn wanted to confirm that his handiwork worked before deploying it in full. Farrier had largely been a soloist since the secret society had split up, but he was grateful for the connection. "Tell me about this thing," he said to Washburn.

"What's there to tell?" Washburn replied. "It's the low end." As if that explained any of it. Memories were filtering back into Farrier's head, now. He recalled enjoying Washburn's company in small doses, but also felt the capacity for shame erupt in those bygone moments.

And so Washburn took out binoculars and took sight of a suit-clad man in a distant window. On the car's central console was a small rectangle, a home-brewed thing with an antenna attached to it and a button that seemed pilfered from a suburban doorbell.

"Can you push that when I give the signal?" Washburn asked. Farrier assented. "Okay. Now," Washburn said. "Just a tap."

Farrier pressed it, held down for half a second, and released the button.

"Oh yeah," said Washburn. "He doesn't know it yet, but he's going to be real twitchy soon. Gonna feel it in his guts. All types of ripe intestinal distress."

"Who's the guy?" asked Farrier.

"Does it matter?" said Washburn.

Farrier thought for a little bit. He knew that tone; that was the tone of someone who believed themselves to be the smartest person in the room. More specifically, that was the tone of someone who needed to have the last word, and who believed they'd gotten the last word in.

And so Farrier said, "It might."

Washburn's face took on an exasperated cast. "Fine. The guy in there is some finance bro. There was an affair, or something. That guy was the, what's the word, the cuckolder. And so the man who felt betrayed hired me to, you know. Petty revenge."

He looked over at Farrier with a moderate glare.

"That's the fun thing. These finance guys? They pay well. Who knows. Maybe next week this guy up here," and here he indicated the office building in the distance, "will pay me to make his rival feel a profound discomfort. I'm agnostic in these matters."

Farrier saw a small form pacing in the windows in the distance. "All right, Farrier," said Washburn. "You can press the button again. We've got proof of concept." And so Farrier did, and they were off.

Five days of being Washburn's second had Farrier pondering drowning his old acquaintance in a nearby river. Not really, but he could see it getting to that point before long. Most of Washburn's work was similar to the first task they'd undertaken: something petty, paid for by someone with too much disposable income. Weird science as the plaything of the idle rich; it was enough to make the largely apolitical Farrier an ardent Marxist, chiming in for class war, storming the barricades, and eventually devouring the affluent.

Still, it paid. Farrier was not exactly someone with a skill set that translated well to traditional resumes and job applications. Washburn had offered him a space on his futon, but Farrier had politely declined. The eight to ten hours they saw one another daily was all he could stand of that dynamic, and he was unsure what prolonging it might do. Cue the aforementioned river and the aforementioned drowning. So instead he spent his time at some sort of extended-stay hotel, a departure from his usual practice, and one that left him feeling off-kilter. Specifically, he had the sense that he had broken into the kitchen and living room and bathroom of someone with decidedly anonymous taste, and had a persistent anxiety that this deeply boring human would some day unlock the door, step inside, and say to Farrier, "And just who the fuck are you?"

Of course, if Farrier opted to remake his old product, he could potentially become that very boring person. He would look at himself in the mirror and see someone other than Farrier. At times, that prospect seemed very inviting.

~13~

In his downtime Farrier circulated among the small towns in Pittsburgh's orbit. Here he found decent food, quiet speciality shops, and a good second-run movie theater. One night he went there for a late show of *Forbidden Planet*. It was a welcome night. He felt sustained by these towns. It did strike him as strange, but he valued that sense of being somewhere between anonymity and regularity.

There was a coffee shop he'd begun to frequent for his breakfasts as well. Driscoll Bridge Coffee was its name; it was in a modest A-frame house that had been hollowed out and transformed into a spacious place to absorb the morning. The strange thing about it, at least for Farrier, was the fact that it was the twin of an identically-named establishment that he'd encountered six years before, outside of Tacoma. Same name, same aesthetic, same sensibility.

It wasn't just a similarity — more than anything else, Farrier felt as though he was back in that original place, that he had somehow opened a door in the northeast and ended up in the northwest. It was a bizarre and very specific shortcut, and he savored it, and the sense that he had someone eluded a basic law of physics quietly thrilled him. He savored this indifferent defiance. He asked once if they had some connection. They did not, and yet he still wondered if he'd step out of the door and into a different state, a different climate, a different now.

☆☆

His eighth gig with Washburn took them across the state line into Ohio. "You know I don't like cities," Farrier said.

"We won't be there for long," said Washburn.

Their drive on the interstate was quiet. On this particular morning Washburn wasn't much of a talker, and Farrier had never been much of a talker. His default mode for driving long distances was solitude, and he'd learned to embrace the sights around him even when he wasn't behind the wheel.

They pulled into an airport hotel and parked. "Here?" said Farrier.

"Here," said Washburn.

They walked inside. Washburn wasn't carrying anything, which struck Farrier as strange. Washburn usually had a case with him that contained at least one piece of obscure audio gear. Washburn headed for the hotel's restaurant and Farrier followed suit.

Awaiting them at a sparse round table was a thin man with a conical head topped with a shock of prematurely graying hair. Farrier knew this look: the eyes of someone fully self-confident, curdled to the point of arrogance. He'd largely seen it around his own associates, his old cohorts in the secret society. They had cultivated themselves with tech millionaires. They had plugged themselves into that world and seamlessly segued into that world when their paths had parted ways with Farrier's. They had embraced the technologist's life and he had remained something like an exile.

Then again, his old cohorts were legitimate and he was here, living and working in these bizarre shadows, most of the way towards being an outlaw.

The shock-headed man was named Nault. Washburn made the introductions and bade Farrier sit. Nault's problem, he explained, was an old one. Seven years before he founded a company called Trials By Fire LLC. The company had been slightly profitable in its first year of business, more profitable in its second year of business, and thoroughly profitable in the years since then. All of that, he thoroughly embraced.

Early on, Nault had had a business partner named Newell. During the slightly profitable year and the decidedly profitable year, there had been, as per Nault's expression, some corners cut. There had been some things done that might be, as per Nault's expression, frowned upon in certain circles. He knew where the bodies were buried. And here, Nault stressed that this was not to be taken literally. Now Nault feared for the future of Trials By Fire LLC.

"Hence," said Nault, and indicated Washburn and, after another beat, Farrier.

"Hence us," said Washburn.

"To help with the problem," said Nault.

"Yes indeed," said Washburn.

"In what way," said Farrier, who immediately realized that he shouldn't have spoken.

Nault smirked. "You have your talents, I'm sure." Farrier was not one to dislike someone on sight, but Nault was rapidly becoming an exception. There was something about him that left Farrier fuming. There was something about the way he had outsourced this impossible problem to Washburn and, by extension, to Farrier that left him spent. Had he once found this life glamorous? He couldn't remember.

"You'll keep this all untraceable," Nault said. "All within the bounds of the law. All deftly handled." And Washburn nodded. After a moment, Farrier realized that he should also nod, that Nault expected it, and so he nodded, quickly but definitively.

"Good good," he said. "Quick like a bunny. Thank you, gentlemen." He stood and shook Washburn's hand and passed Farrier by. "Good day," he said, and walked out of the restaurant of the airport hotel.

Washburn regarded Farrier with borrowed contempt. "Be nicer to him if we meet him again."

"Do you think we will?" said Farrier.

"You need to be nicer to him."

"I don't see any reason why we have to. Why I have to."

"God damn it Farrier," Washburn said. "Say you'll be nice to the man. Deferential. Respectful. Or I'll strand you at this place and dump your car in the river when I get home."

The worst thing about it was the flat tone, Farrier thought. Washburn seemed robotic, a programmatic sense of misplaced devotion. And while he understood the mechanics of it — Washburn had relationships with his clients, while the nature of Farrier's work made things a one-off each time — he didn't have to like it. Nault was showing dominance to Washburn and Washburn was showing dominance to him and he didn't particularly care for either.

Of course, what he said was simpler. "I'll be nicer to him."

"Good," Washburn said, and then paused. Let the point sink in, apparently. Lovely, thought Farrier.

"So what is the plan?" Farrier asked.

"You don't have any brain shit that we can use on him, do you?" Washburn said.

"I do not," said Farrier. This wasn't strictly true, but he had no desire to use the last of the product on this endeavor. "Why, though? Sonics won't do the trick here?"

"I think this gig calls for more than just discomfort," said Washburn. "Here, we need full-on transformation. Or conversion. Embracing the ecstatic, or the demonic."

110

"Maybe we should just send a priest over," said Farrier. "Someone who'll quote scripture and verse to this Newell guy until he cracks, checks himself into a monastic order, and never leaves."

"Convent is nuns," said Washburn. "Abbey is monks."

"Same thing," Farrier said. "Same intention. Celibacy and chanting, and sometimes they make ale."

They left the restaurant soon afterwards and spent the drive back to the outskirts of Pittsburgh discussing a plan. The talk continued at Washburn's office and went on well into the night. Plans were arranged and rearranged. And in the midst of this, Farrier made his own plans, something that slipped inside of Washburn's blueprints like a diver into a suit.

Nils Newell was enthusiastically eccentric. He had a penchant for customizing luxurious tents and had sunk minor fortunes into nominally bizarre yet successful business endeavors. After traveling extensively in Australia and India, he had seen abundant emu farms there and had decided that, by God, this would be the way in which he expanded his fortune. Even more bizarre than that conviction was the fact that it had worked. Nils Newell's net worth was now somewhere in the mid-eight figures, and he was a notable socialite in certain circles. During the rest of the year he could be found at his estate, either in one of the buildings there or sprawled languorously in a tent. For all of his many quirks, he had a firm reputation for honesty, and was largely admired by those whom he encountered. Though certainly not everyone he encountered; otherwise, there would be no reason for Washburn and Farrier to be on the case.

Behold, then: the plan of action. Washburn had been tasked with turning Newell into a pariah, leaving him vulnerable to the rapacity of his stockholders and the inevitable fuckery of late capitalism. Newell had taken his company public and was now pondering a move to reverse that decision, and Washburn's client wanted an annulment of the reversal. Thus the hiring of Washburn; thus the belief in precise discretion and bizarre science.

Newell lived on a massive farm on the outskirts of nowhere. The previous occupant had been the favorite scion of some reclusive investor, who'd been given tips and tricks to make the world of markets and machinations malleable. The former occupant had spent the last decade of his life enmeshed in legal skirmishes with state and federal authorities. And while their efforts to entrap and ensnare him hadn't entirely worked, it had made him increasingly more cognizant of his own moral failings. To that end, he'd poisoned himself one October evening, leaving his body propped up in a field, akin to a scarecrow if seen from a distance. It had taken a few weeks before someone finally noticed that this solitary figure was something other than a practical tool for crow mitigation or a decoration for the forthcoming holiday.

The saga of this farm had been documented in an acclaimed work of nonfiction. The book had been optioned for film and a screenplay had been written, but that was as far as it had reached. But a crusading radio producer had embraced the story and transformed it into a podcast; this podcast had become somewhat infamous, and this podcast was the soundtrack to Washburn and Farrier's stakeouts of the Newell estate. Farrier, at least, enjoyed the cyclical nature of it. For his part, Washburn would just shake his head dubiously at various points in the narrative. "They got hosed," he'd say. "They all got hosed." He never quite mentioned who "they" were. Farrier wasn't sure that it mattered.

Driving in seemed impossible; so too did flying in, or borrowing a drone and hoping that it could soar over spacious fields undetected. "Tunneling?" Farrier half-heartedly suggested, which was met with a contemptuous glare from Washburn.

The estate wasn't a fortress per se, but it was sprawling enough that an unknown car or truck would be instantly noticeable. Farrier and Washburn sat in a car on an adjacent street spinning wild theories of how they might enter — disguises, pest control, a false burglary, a real burglary, art appraisers, county employees, security consultants, nouveau riche scum, journalists, technologists, erotic seismologists, or perhaps simply as themselves, offering their services to him as a cover for doing his rival's work. Nothing quite seemed to fit.

In the end Washburn came up with a solution. Farrier realized at that moment that Washburn would have always been the one to come up with the solution. They would undermine Newell's car; they would use the car as their means of insidiously rattling Newell, thus arriving at their goal.

"We'll set out for it tomorrow," Washburn said, and that was that.

Thirty-six hours later, Washburn nursed the burn on his left forearm and sipped from a snifter of sufficient whiskey. "The car might not be the way to go after all," he said.

Farrier held the ice pack to his forehead and hoped his eye was less bloodshot than it had been three hours ago. "Washburn," he said. "I think the car is out. Look at me. Look at us. If we had three or four other people, maybe. But we don't."

Washburn nodded and growled his assent, a low throaty sound that uncannily evoked a positive assonance. "Well all right," he said. "Can you think of another weak spot?"

Farrier had, as it turned out. Newell's mansion was a converted farmhouse. The previous owners had added onto it gradually and, praise be, organically. They had not sought to demolish it, nor had they thought to completely remake it. Rather, they had simply let it sprawl; they had upgraded certain components with higher-quality materials, but they had opted for something palatial rather than something extravagant. It was a small definition, Farrier understood, but one worth making.

And the building that had once been a small barn, with a few stalls and a large hayloft, had long ago been turned into a library, in which Newell spent some of his hours. His "thinking-brain time," he had called it in one interview. In the profile that Farrier had read, Newell had posed with a selection of leather-bound tomes behind him, not a speck of dust to be seen on the spines of the books or the shoulders of their owner.

"We can't get into the house," said Farrier. "But I'm pretty sure the library is up for grabs." He studied Washburn's face carefully. Washburn was the sort of man who would give you three-quarters of an idea, but not any more. That was what Farrier had handed off to him: the nascent seed of something, Washburn would seize on this riff and, like some ecstatic jazz musician, embrace it and turn into something personal and strange. This was how Washburn collaborated.

The brainstorming session ended twenty minutes later on an ambiguous note. This was fine by Farrier. He retreated to his hotel's bar and got alarmingly drunk and spent the following morning raiding the hotel's breakfast spread for anything involving eggs and cheese. He suspected that Washburn was in one of his moods, that he'd gone to ground somewhere, to turn over this germ of an idea that Farrier had passed off. Farrier assumed he'd hear from Washburn in about a day and a half. He decided to keep to himself for the next day and a half. This was Washburn's city, after all. He sometimes felt like an invasive species here. He was already beginning to ponder his way out.

On the morning after Farrier's hangover morning, Washburn called. "I'll pick you up at eleven," he said. "Wear something classy."

"I don't have anything classy," Farrier replied. "This isn't a line of work where I go to black-tie events."

Farrier could picture Washburn's look of disappointment. "Fucking fine," Washburn said. "There's a menswear store at the mall. Tailoring on the premises. We'll head there. Bring cash."

It seemed to Farrier that malls were like urban downtowns designed by aliens who'd never visited cities. You had the density, you had the retail and the food, you had the pedestrian fixation, but you also had something else, something inherently distancing. There was a sense of place and also a fundamental divorce from any specific place. This was what he thought, at least, as they stood in the mall on the outskirts of the Pittsburgh metropolitan area.

They had gone to a menswear store, just as Washburn had promised. A surly Russian-accented man had greeted them, had nodded brusquely to Washburn, and had gone about taking Farrier's measurements. Farrier wondered if Washburn had brought a legion of ersatz sidekicks here over the years, donning each in dapper suits before leading each to some form of sacrifice. Sacrifice? he asked himself. Apparently the Rust Belt had turned him morbid.

The suit most readily available was dark blue. The menswear adjutant produced a series of shirts and asked Farrier if he had a preference between cufflinks and an absence of cufflinks. Farrier opted for the latter, to Washburn's visible dismay. "What?" said Farrier. "Fewer moving parts."

"Fine," said Washburn. "I'm trying to maintain a certain air of class over here with this operation."

Farrier began to answer, then thought better of it. He handed over payment for the suit, two shirts, and a pair of nondescript dress shoes. They went back out to Washburn's car and drove back to the hotel and he changed and they returned to Washburn's car and the road.

"So what's the plan?"

"We're impersonating rare book dealers and staking out the Newell library. We have a 4 pm appointment."

"Better than a 4 am appointment."

Washburn glared at him. "You'd be surprised. These rich guys are into weird shit like that." He looked back at the road for a second, cleared his throat, and said again, "You'd be surprised."

The Newell library was suitably glorious. If you looked closely enough you could see the shadows of the structure's former use: certain joints and bits of wood that served no purpose in a library, but which clearly connected some structural seams during its previous iteration. That was the tricky thing about spaces such as this, Farrier thought. Those old bits never quite went away. Except, of course, when it came to his own work.

Farrier walked around the resplendent room and jotted down notes, nominally about titles and areas of interest but actually focusing more on hiding spaces, acoustics, the architectural acrostics that could bring this space towards an unlikely revelation. He wasn't sure exactly how Washburn had successfully created a book dealer cover story in such a short time. Perhaps Washburn had had one all along; perhaps that was his own clever talent. Either way, Farrier circled the room again and again until he felt thoroughly intimate with it.

He kept an eye on Washburn, who was in conversation with someone representing Newell's holdings. Assumably this was the person who controlled the flow of money, who dispensed and retracted access at the estate's gate, who advised immeasurably well and welcomed new clients with a handshake and a careful management of necessary information. The majordomo, then.

Farrier had had a majordomo for a client once, in his past life. This man had been, apparently, tremendous in his job, a tireless advocate for his employer and someone who pushed themselves to their limits for the sake of a paycheck and a solid appraisal. And thus he had reached his breaking point, having determined his particular talent involved the abnegation of himself for the sake of someone else, and that this would eventually leave himself so utterly spent that he might simply become a machine, a fictive device to benefit someone else. "I can't imagine doing anything else," this man had told Farrier, "but I also can't imagine this not being my utter ruin." And Farrier had nodded and had sold him the product, and that concluded their interaction. Farrier watched this new majordomo talk with Washburn and hoped that their self of work and life was more assured.

After forty minutes of pacing the room and taking careful notes, Farrier saw Washburn shake hands with the majordomo. Washburn beckoned him over. "Our day is done," said Washburn, and they walked towards Washburn's car. They were silent as they drove through the fields of the Newell estate, past the large house in which Newell himself dwelled, and finally out of the gate and past the small guardhouse that controlled access in and out.

Farrier turned to Washburn, opening his notes as he did. "So we've got options," Farrier said. "We have plenty of options, depending on what you want to do."

Washburn had a smirk on his face. "You know, I think we can go low-tech on this one."

Farrier was bemused. "How so?"

"I don't think we need my tech here. Or your tech. I think we should just burn the place down."

And to that, Farrier was silent.

⁑

Farrier and Washburn reconvened three hours later at a bar and restaurant in the middle of nowhere. The outside was covered in logs, looking like nothing quite so much as a frontier home. Inside, though, was interchangeable: cheap beer, sports posters, hideous well whiskey, and a small stage set up on which, Farrier assumed, someone would loudly play cover songs later in the night. Farrier hoped they'd be gone by then but he wouldn't put it past Washburn to keep them there for the entirety of the set. Farrier remembered working with Washburn years before; a part of their gig had involved staking out a bowling alley in central New Jersey, and they sat in a room as someone standing before a keyboard energetically and badly sang rock anthems while a couple slowly ground their bodies into one another on the de facto dance floor. It had been the singer, the couple, the bartender, and Washburn and Farrier in there. Not for the first time, Farrier wondered about Washburn's voyeurism. At least he'd been spared it so far this time around.

"So can we talk about the burning?" said Farrier.

"What's there to say?" said Washburn. "There are glorious things we can do with drones. Not even needing to bring our skills to the table. Just hovering over the space and dropping things and watching as they combine."

"I thought the gist of this was to be more nebulous."

"Nebulous? You do like the five-dollar words."

"How about 'subtle'?"

Washburn was eating chicken wings. He'd opted for some utterly putrid topping: the sort of thing Farrier wouldn't have eaten on a potato chip, much less on deep-fried meat. His reaction to Farrier's citation of the word "subtle" was to pause, then eat his way through his current wing, then pause, pick up a second wing, and devour that as well. He removed a napkin from the brick-sized stack their server had left and wiped his hands and mouth with it, then drummed his fingers on the edge of the table.

"Subtle is fine. But there's also a question of time. If we're meant to be ghosts here, tormenting him with our rattling chains — look, I can use a metaphor, too — that's going to take time. And I have another gig booked in Bar Harbor soon, and the last thing I want to do is depart for the hallowed shores of New England with Newell's facilities intact."

"So instead we do the quick trauma."

Washburn did the drumming motion again. "Precisely," he said.

This was Farrier's quandary: he could make his case, or even offer to stay on in western Pennsylvania and resolve this solo, though that seemed like it heralded corruption and disgrace. But he also knew that Washburn had set his mind to this and would be nearly impossible to sway. Similarly, he feared Washburn's machinations and syndicates; Washburn was barely tolerating him here, and the fact that this was the first he'd heard of Washburn's Maine assignation struck him as significant in several supporting ways.

So instead he acquiesced to Washburn's plan. And, when Washburn left for the bathroom, he dissolved the remains of his last dosage of the product in Washburn's whiskey.

When Washburn returned from the washroom, Farrier wondered if this was it. But Washburn was pompous rather than paranoid, and sniftered back the remains of his whiskey in one gulp. "That does it for me," he said. "Keep it going here tonight if you want, but I'm out."

"I think I'll have one more," said Farrier. "Some calm before the storm."

"Well all right," said Washburn. "A pleasure imbibing with you."

"Surely," said Farrier.

And that was it. Washburn walked to the door and out the door, and that was it. Farrier sat and ordered another beer and slowly drank it, waiting for Washburn to burst back through or for his phone to ring or for a telltale text with "I KNOW WHAT YOU DID AND I STOPPED IT" emblazoned across the front of his phone. None of these things came.

When the server brought the tip he realized that Washburn had stuck him with the bill. Under other circumstances he'd have been angry. Here, he was merely relieved. He was surprised, in the end, that he had it in him. But still: it had been done. He drove back to his hotel, packed up his room, and headed south.

~14~

He drove for fourteen hours on southward diagonals after leaving Pittsburgh. There was one bolt-hole left to him, and it was there that he was bound. He would be there in just over a day of constant motion — so, two long days of driving punctuated by a hotel somewhere. The trick of this drive was that it was neither the most scenic route nor the most efficient. He didn't think Washburn would fight off his stupor for long enough to mount a pursuit, but neither did he want to test that notion. And so, the open road.

In a rest stop in western Ohio he saw a woman who resembled a neighbor he'd crushed on in high school, and at a rest stop near the border of Illinois and Indiana he would have sworn that he saw an old college professor, and at a rest stop somewhere in Missouri he saw a familiar face and a familiar outline and then remembered that the man conjured by this shape and this face was long dead.

Farrier hated seeing ghosts on the road, even if they weren't actually ghosts. Seeing ghosts on the road usually meant it was time for a break. He found a hotel near St. Robert that had a notable breakfast bar and he booked a room and carried his remaining possessions in a suitcase up to that room and sat in the room and showered in the room and slept a long and unhelpful sleep. No specters haunted his sleep; none came to his room to watch him slumber.

All of his dreams that night were of driving, but here the landscapes were all wrong. Herds of strange and displaced animals clustered by the sides of the roads as he drove along. Sometimes his back seat was full of luggage and sometimes it was empty and sometimes there was someone back there, someone comfortable and familiar, silent save their breathing. Some truant from his conscious life.

In his dreams he drove across continents without names. In the waking world, his routes were much more mundane.

He made good time the following day and was in Texas an hour and a half ahead of schedule. He'd made it to Colorado City by the time he saw the clouds on the horizon, moving in from the south and west. They were grey and loomed overhead and looked like the end of days. Farrier had never been much for forecasts; he had driven in blizzards and through torrential downpours, though he hadn't enjoyed either. But something about the tinge of these clouds gave him pause. He pulled into the city's downtown, fighting a sense of unease throughout.

Farrier found a coffee shop and ordered something and looked at the weather and saw news of a hurricane heading from his destination to his location. Farrier finished his coffee and darted back to his car, drove to the closest hotel, and holed up for the night. Ten minutes after checking in he heard the sound of rain falling in cascades from outside. Good decisions had been rare for him lately, but he was proud of this one.

On the roadside near the hotel was a building labeled THE MUSEUM OF UNTRUTH. Farrier was intrigued, truth be told, despite his sneaking suspicion that this was some sort of lure to get him to witness something religious. He had been bait-and-switched in this manner before, and the unsure shock of being asked to stand and chant along with the devout still stung.

Anyway, it was a moot point. Before the downpours resumed Farrier walked outside and crossed the hotel's parking lot and entered the museum's parking lot over some imperceptible divide. He surveyed the building: it was repurposed from some older purpose, perhaps a dental office or a warehouse or a Carnegie library. And on the window, the phrase "the Museum of Untruth" had been etched in a script that, to Farrier's eyes, looked thoroughly secular. Still, he felt a pang of disappointment, as directly below that was a neatly printed logo explaining that the museum was closed for renovation.

For a moment Farrier wondered if he should perhaps break in. He assumed the downpour would reduce any potential police response and, since his time with Washburn, he'd felt a lessening of his moral compass. Even so, he balked at this. He would make a note of this place, he told himself. He would pass by it again on some journey, for some purpose. Some version of his life would enable this to work out. There was nothing more to regret, he told himself. There was only a future full of potential.

~15~

Farrier fell asleep shortly after the first raindrops started to fall. He woke once in the middle of the night, his stomach nauseous. He sat at the edge of the bed and listened to the steady showers from outside and waited for the feeling of discomfort to subside. He glanced over at the alarm on the night table and saw that it was 4:17. He looked through the blinds and the blackout curtains and saw a steady downpour outside, simple sheets of rain falling unceasingly. He used to welcome rain like this; it would herald the end of succulent humidity or hearken the conclusion of a dry spell. Having been here for very little time, and having spent nearly all of it in climate-controlled environments, Farrier had no idea which of these this was. He stared out at the parking lots and the buildings beyond, all rendered indistinct by the rain, until he again felt the pull of sleep and returned to the bed.

When he woke again and looked at the clock he saw that it was eleven. The air and light in the room seemed little changed from when he had awakened seven hours earlier. He walked back to the windows and again drew back the blinds and the blackout curtains. There was little more light now than there had been in the early morning. The rain still fell across the parking lot at the same relentless velocity. Farrier was glad that he had booked this room for several days, and wondered if he would need to extend his stay even longer.

Farrier showered and put on clean clothes and walked down to the lobby. He availed himself of the complimentary coffee and looked around. Aside from the clerk behind the desk there was no one else there. Outside it looked like twilight; outside it looked like no particular time, either an endless night or a perennial no-time, a missing part of the day or a sum total of the daylight and the night.

Farrier walked to the desk. The man who stood behind it was college-aged and well-groomed. Farrier gestured at the empty lobby. "Slow time of year?" he asked.

The clerk shook his head. "Usually we're packed this week," he said. "Weather threw a wrench in that, though. Storm coming up from the west caused a bunch of events to be postponed, and thus we ended up with...a lot of nothing."

"Good for me, I guess."

"More than likely," said the clerk. "Without this rain, there'd have been no vacancies here, or probably anywhere for a good fifty miles."

"Jesus," said Farrier.

"Lots of outdoor things this time of year," said the clerk. "A blessing and a curse."

Farrier could relate.

"So," said the clerk. "You were on your way somewhere?"

"Yeah," said Farrier. "Somewhere west. Long trip, visiting people. Something like that." Sometimes Farrier didn't feel the need to be distinct with his language. He wagered that this conversation was one of those times. The clerk didn't seem to take offense, so Farrier assumed he was correct.

"So what's there to do around here?" Farrier asked.

The clerk laughed. "I'm guessing you don't feel like driving?" Farrier shook his head. "Do you have an umbrella?" Farrier indicated that he did not. "Well then," said the clerk. "There's a restaurant attached to here that opens for lunch in half an hour, and there's a bar at the other end of the first floor that opens up at four."

"How's the food?" asked Farrier.

"It's not bad, if you like cheese. But if you don't like cheese, you're out of luck."

"And how's the bar?"

"Bar's good," said the clerk. "If I didn't work here I'd go there. It's also the spot open latest around these parts, so — it's a blend of folks. Your guests and your locals. Can be fun, can be feisty."

Briefly, Farrier wondered if this was a euphemism for something more sinister or salacious, but concluded that it was not.

"It's much appreciated," said Farrier. "One more thing, though."

"Yes indeed," said the clerk.

"My reservation is through tomorrow. If I want to extend that, is that a possibility?"

The clerk chuckled. "This place is a ghost town for the next week," he said. "You'll be fine."

Farrier smiled. "All right," he said. "I'll let you know after lunch."

He returned to his room before lunch to survey what he still had with him. He could run current through his brain, and he had a rudimentary amount of chemicals and substances that he could form into something that might have an effect on his head. Still, this was no lab; his options were limited. He stared at it all and moved items from table to table and rearranged them in various combinations. Finch had warned him about this: she had told him once that he'd go full mad scientist some day, and now it was coming to pass in a hotel room in West Texas.

These were his devices: the generator that spiked electricity to electrodes that he could mount on his forehead; a mortar and pestle, for the cruder works; a handful of pills with varying psychological effects; six notebooks full of calculations and summations, the piecework research that had gotten him to the point of the product; four bottles of various distillates and solutions that would likely alter his brain chemistry in some bizarre way or ways, but which did not lend themselves to prediction; a tablet on which he maintained records of the recipients of the product; a journal in which he tested theories about other uses for his knowledge; five psychedelic mushrooms; one small bottle of vodka in which a sixth psychedelic mushroom soaked; two books by Terence McKenna; a diary kept by one of the recipients of the drug documenting their experience of changing; four empty flasks; a jar of pill casings; an 1813 tome on botany; a self-portrait; a guide to terrestrial handwriting; a photograph of the old secret society, before it had all gone to shit. Mementoes and materials and evidence.

He could make himself a reasonable facsimile of the product from these components, he thought. Not something suitable for a client, but something private for his own use, or his potential use.

He put it together, less out of a desire to try it than as a way to spend the time. Hours passed, and eventually he went back down to the lobby in search of the bar. The same clerk was there who had been there before. "Remind me," said Farrier. "Where do I go to get to the bar?"

The clerk pointed off to one side. "It's a long trek, I'll be honest. Be on the lookout for the space-age materials. They're quite fancy, I'm told."

"I do like science," said Farrier.

"Well then," said the clerk. "It's your lucky day."

And so Farrier bade him farewell and walked in the indicated direction. He passed through an archway, the kind of thing that one might pass through in a biodome, or in a botanical garden, or in a complex and streamlined aquarium. The materials did indeed look futuristic, if not new: it struck Farrier that this walkway was someone's idea of state of the art at one point, though it likely was no longer. Above him Farrier saw the walls of the hotel and an endless graph of closed windows, the dim blue of the sky reflected in them. Soon enough it would again be night. Farrier had no desire to go out in what remained of the day, especially not with more storms looming.

The passageway reached its end, terminating in a round room that evoked nothing quite so much as a large geodesic dome. Perhaps, viewed from the outside, that was what it was. Neon strips clung to the walls and gave the room a hazy, delirious look. There were a host of televisions mounted on the walls, all of which were off. There were booths and tables and chairs spaced evenly around the room, none of which were occupied. And there were a series of stools lined up adjacent to the bar, all of which were empty. The space behind the bar, too, was empty. Farrier pulled up a stool and waited.

He slipped into a fugue, where the low hum of the neon and the subdued lights of the room combined and left him feeling as though he had already slipped into night, and that night had turned endless.

He checked the time and saw that he had been waiting there for thirty-five minutes. That was enough for him to conclude that the bartender was simply absent, and he crossed back through the long tunnel to the front desk. As he walked, he could hear the downpour's steady tattoo impacting it and impacting it and impacting it all over again.

Back to the concourse. Back to the clerk. "So," said Farrier, and the clerk knew instantly that would come next.

"No barman," said the clerk.

"No barman," said Farrier.

"So apparently he quit," said the clerk. "Called my manager with the news just after you walked towards the bar."

"Well, shit," said Farrier. "And there's no one to spell him?"

The clerk shook his head, then laughed. "You're not up for making a little extra cash, are you?" he said. "Because there's going to be a need for someone behind the bar tonight. Cabin fever for those guests staying inside the hotel and no easy way to get a replacement in. It's bad out there, in case you hadn't noticed."

Farrier thought about it. He was reasonably sure that he could handle the requests made by the guests and staff of a hotel bar. "Why not?" he said.

The clerk handed him a couple of forms and Farrier signed them. This was his first official act in years. It felt strange. Still, this brought with it a sense of purpose. "Is what I'm wearing all right for the gig?" Farrier asked.

"Probably not," said the clerk. "But for right now, who cares?"

And so Farrier walked back under the arches of the passageway. He'd kept the version of the product he'd assembled earlier on his person, and in this space he withdrew it from his pocket. He looked at it for as long as he could without attracting stares. This one probably wouldn't remake him entirely, but it might have some similar effect. Perhaps he would soon no longer be Farrier, but instead be some new version of himself. Tomorrow, he would telephone Finch; he would start another secret society, perhaps. He would call this place home. He would tend bar and have his hidden lair somewhere nearby and unlock the secrets of the mind and understand the nature of the self. Or he would do none of these things, and would simply grow old here, an aging bartender with no other concerns, making a life from mixing dry martinis for tourists and football fans. Any of these lives seemed acceptable to him. He had the product on his person; he could use it at any time. Perhaps in an hour or two he would.

Farrier stepped behind the bar, adopted a slightly rakish manner, and waited for the first customers to arrive. He wondered what his shift might bring, and what the results of his efforts to reach out might be. He wondered if his dreams would be different tonight. He wondered if after tonight, his dreams would belong to someone else. So began this night.

IN THE SIGHT

ABOUT THE AUTHOR

Tobias Carroll is a writer and essayist, and the managing editor of *Vol. 1 Brooklyn*. In addition to *In the Sight*, he is the author of: *Political Sign* (Bloomsbury), part of the *Object Lessons* series; the story collection *Transitory* (Civil Coping Mechanisms); the novel *Reel* (Rare Bird); and the novel *Ex-Members* (Astrophil).

ABOUT THE PUBLISHER

Whisk(e)y Tit is committed to restoring degradation and degeneracy to the literary arts. We work with authors who are unwilling to sacrifice intellectual rigor, unrelenting playfulness, and visual beauty in our literary pursuits, often leading to texts that would otherwise be abandoned in today's largely homogenized literary landscape. In a world governed by idiocy, our commitment to these principles is an act of civil service and civil disobedience alike.